AMARANTHINE
RAIN

a short story collection

Zander Vyne

AMARANTHINE RAIN

by Zander Vyne

FULL SAIL PUBLISHING

Published in the United States by Full Sail Publishing.
Cover and page design by DJ at JustWrite Design.

Printed in the United States.
©2016 Zander Vyne.

ISBN-10: 0-9910823-4-6
ISBN-13: 978-0-9910823-4-6

This is a work of fiction. Names, characters, places, media, and incidents are either the product of the author's imagination or are used fictitiously.

Table of Contents

IN THE NAME OF THE FATHER

Every Sunday Isabella came to see Michael and, after her visits, the lingering scent of her haunted him— sandalwood, jasmine, and something else elusively female. He wanted to ask her what it was. Truthfully, he wanted to buy it and dribble it on his pillows so he could sleep with her, if only in his dreams.

But, that was impossible, so he struggled to banish his fantasies and concentrate on other things; he tried to do his job. His cock throbbed, though, each time she was near. He couldn't do a thing about that.

Sometimes, he could see only bits of her face; in here, she was shadowed and mysterious. He'd summon images of her dark beauty in other settings and place them over the veiled person actually in front of him on Sundays. He liked to think of her in the sunshine, outside. He'd never seen her that way—her brown hair shining, her full mouth smiling and laughing. He liked to imagine her happy and not as she was when she spent time with him.

"Antonio had him killed. I heard them talking about it. They didn't know I was in the kitchen, and they laughed.

They laughed," Isabella said.

"You must go to the police." Michael knew she wouldn't, even as he said it; they'd had similar conversations before.

He'd also talked with several of the women Isabella's husband kept on the side. They all feared Antonio Moretti too, though unlike Isabella, they also craved what his power, his influence, and his money could do for them.

Isabella wasn't like them. She'd actually loved Tony when they'd married, years ago. Now, all she wanted was to escape him.

"You know I can't do that."

Michael sighed, curling his fingers around his cross. Surely, this was a test. Only trouble was he had no desire to pass it. What he wanted was to take Isabella away from anything that hurt her. He wanted to rescue her. He wanted to fuck her.

God help him.

He'd been a priest for only a few months and had never fallen in the face of enticement, even as a typical, randy teenager. There'd been a lot of temptation; he'd grown up in Southern California, surrounded by girls in bikinis and suntan oil. One of the first things he had to confess was almost wearing his palms out jerking off. Of course, he'd been forgiven and, since taking the sacrament, he'd kept his promise to God.

He was a twenty-five year old virgin, by choice.

Since Isabella had walked into his confessional, Michael had started to regret his decision not to walk on the wild side before becoming a servant of the Lord. Many of the other men had made sure of the calling by fucking anything that moved in the weeks before making it final, but Michael had remained devout. Now he questioned the wisdom of that choice and toyed almost daily with the idea of giving in to the overwhelming temptations Isabella offered.

Surely Eve herself couldn't have been more enticing than Isabella. Though she was old enough to be his mother, there was something ripe about her, something fresh and sensual. Her figure was rounded, yet firm looking. Her legs were elegant and slinky in the expensive looking skirts and dresses she always wore. She was ladylike in her heels, with her long hair usually pulled back into a twist. Michael wondered what it would look like loose. He imagined it caressing the curves of her bare hips. He imagined her in white, cotton underwear.

There was something almost Madonna-like in Isabella's sad brown eyes, but more and more, the things she said told Michael she was more Mary Magdalene than the Virgin Mary.

He ached to save her.

At first, they'd spoken only of Isabella's "normal" sins— bad thoughts, little white lies (she really was a good Catholic). During Mass, she always ignored Michael completely, but over time, in the shadowed privacy of the confessional, she told him of her life, her hopes, her horrors, and her desires.

She asked too, about his life, how he'd come to be here, where he'd come from. No one else had ever stopped talking about themselves long enough to ask about him. He was surprised to find he had a lot to say. Each week he cared for her a little more. It became difficult, listening to her talk about her private hell.

Everyone in the parish knew Tony beat her. The dark glasses and makeup didn't hide much. But no one knew the things Isabella shared with Michael about the vile behavior she suffered in the bedroom. No one knew the turmoil she lived with every day, knowing exactly what Tony's "business" was, but powerless to change anything.

"Just once, I want to know what it's like to have someone

hold me with love and touch me like a woman. Is that so wrong, Father? Is it?"

"No, Isabella, it's human," Michael said, a sickening feeling in his gut as he imagined anyone touching her.

He had a crazy fantasy—in the split second it took for her to speak again—of leaving the confessional, grabbing her by the hand, and running far away. Mexico maybe. No way could he kill Tony, no way could they turn him in, but if they could disappear, surely they'd be safe. He'd make love to Isabella in the warm, white sand. He'd make her happy. God would understand.

"I want it to be you," she said, not for the first time. She pressed her cheek to the partition that separated them.

Michael leaned forward, close enough to feel the warmth of her breath on his mouth. He wanted her too.

They pushed the partition open together and linked hands. She leaned into the narrow opening and laid her head on his chest.

"Isabella . . . I can't," Michael said, even as his hands slipped down the abundant curve of her ass. It felt just the way he'd imagined it would, supple and lush under his squeezing fingers.

His cock was so hard. Even through his vestments, he could feel it driving into her belly. He never wore anything underneath. It was too hot; the old Brooklyn church didn't have air conditioning. Michael's prick rose, velvet-steel brushing his belly, the tip weeping already. He'd not come in years. The blood pounded in his ears, gathered in his balls and in his thickening shaft.

Isabella kissed him, her lips grazing the pulse raging in his neck. Her hands found him in his flowing garment. Clasping him, surrounding him, she began to move her fingers up and down.

"I know you want to, Michael."

Just once, he thought. So many sins were greater. Caught up in his heady lust for her, he plunged his hands into her midnight hair, dragging it from its pins, sending glossy locks down her back.

"Let me," she whispered, searching through folds of heavy black fabric until his hands stopped her and fumbled with the hidden zipper, parting it so she could touch his naked flesh.

She held her rosary in her hand; the black beads were cold and hard as she wrapped them around and around the base of his penis.

God forgive me, he thought. He was going to come.

She bent over and he closed his eyes, clenching his fingers and dropping his hands to her breasts. They filled his palms with sweet softness, pliant under the restraint of her bra. It felt like lace. Her nipples were hard points his thumbs were drawn to, over and over again.

"I want—" Her tongue on his cock silenced him. She licked at the pearled drops oozing from him, sliding over the veins and swollen head.

Michael couldn't remember what he wanted anymore; he just reached for her, his knees banging into the lower part of the confessional wall. He tangled his fingers in her hair, drawing her forward through the opening. Her hot mouth engulfed him, her nose brushed the curls on his belly, and he shuddered.

Her hands stroked him as her mouth loved him. The rosary beads held his prick in a noose and kept him from gushing immediately into her mouth. His cock grew and grew, and he experienced it all with a sense of awe. He was doing it, she was doing him, and it was fucking amazing.

Her cock-wet mouth glistened in the dim light as she let his throbbing penis go, her spit-slick hand sliding up and down. She rolled her palm over the head, tickling that little gather of flesh on the underside where he'd been circumcised. His legs shook.

She took him between her lips again and groaned. That was his undoing, he couldn't hold it; he flooded her mouth, jetting deep into her throat. He felt her gag and swallow. It only made it better, the squeeze clamping down on his cock, milking it. He shoved himself into her, his fingers clutching her hair. It was all he could do not to scream.

She looked up at him and licked him clean, sloe-eyed. She dropped her rosary beads into her pocket and stood up, wrapping him in a hug.

"You taste like the sea," she whispered.

His head spun. He clung to her until she pulled away and left the confessional.

The next time Michael saw Isabella was the following Sunday in church. She came to Mass with her husband.

She moved slowly and wore a black veil over her face. Tony held her arm for support. Though to some the gesture might have looked loving, Michael knew otherwise.

He smiled at the older parish ladies, kissed the new babies, and almost ran into the confessional the moment he could escape. He knew Isabella would come; she always did.

He listened to Mona De Leon tell him about stealing a dress from the Woolworth's and told her to take it back, say she was sorry, and do ten Hail Marys.

Johnny Campo had lusted after his sister-in-law, again. Michael suggested a vacation with his wife and gave him passages of the bible to read about faithfulness.

Heather Anderson wanted someone to whip her and then fuck her silly. She wondered if that was a sin in God's eyes. Michael told her no, as long as she did those things with someone decent and kind, who'd not take advantage of her. It'd help if he was her husband, but Michael wasn't in the mood to be too picky today.

Antonio Moretti was next. He carried with him his wife's scent and Michael's insides tightened.

Tony had never come into Michael's confessional before. He was one of the group who seemed to think absolution was preferable when doled out by the more experienced Priest, Father Murphy.

Michael's mind raced. He barely heard Tony's beginning, but did manage to respond with the appropriate, "Bless you."

Tony was a big man with a booming voice and jovial manner, prone to slapping other men on their backs and winking when he spoke as if everyone was sharing in some big joke. Today, he spoke in hushed tones. Michael had to lean forward to hear him.

"I gotta problem, and I don't want nobody to know 'bout it," Tony said.

"Your confession is sacred," Michael answered. His hands were clenched so tightly his fingernails bit into his palms.

"See, okay . . . it's my wife."

Michael listened, the hairs on the back of his neck prickling.

"This is shameful, Father." Tony sighed and, for a long while, there was nothing but the sound of his breathing.

Michael waited him out.

"Okay, see, I try to be a good husband, to treat her right, you know, in God's way, but the thing is, it's not always so easy."

"Marriage is a challenge," Michael said, wanting to add, "You fucking asshole," but he didn't.

"That's the thing, Father. I try to fuc . . . uh, have relations with her, you know, like missionaries, but she wants it rough and sometimes like a boy, capiche? Now I know the bible says she's a sinful woman, but I kinda like her that way and figure what happens in our house can't be bad in God's eyes if the bitch wants it, right? So, my problem is, well a couple things really, but first I gotta know if I am gonna burn for her, you know, in hell?"

Michael wanted to smash his hand through the partition separating them and slam it into Tony's face. Instead, he took a deep breath and said, very calmly under the circumstances he thought, "No."

"That's it?" Tony laughed, a nasty slithery sound. "You sure are easier than Father Murphy. I shoulda come to you a long time ago. So okay, here's the other thing. See, I think there might be somebody else and, if I find out for sure, I'm gonna kill him with my bare hands. Rip the fucker's heart out. Then I'm gonna make her pay. So like if I did that, it'd be one a them eye for an eye things, right? I could confess and be right with God?"

"No, that would be murder in the Lord's eyes."

"But, the Lord forgives his flock all sins. I only gotta confess it right?"

"Confession is only a part of it." Had he been talking with anyone else, Michael would have explained forethought, intent, contrition, and forgiveness. He'd have talked about the rules of repenting and the wisdom of tolerance. Instead, he just left it at that, praying Tony would leave.

"Okay, Father. I think I got it. You've really been a help."

Michael didn't say another word. He just sat until the door closed behind Tony. Then he listened to all the other confessions, knowing now Isabella wouldn't be in line today.

When Mass was over, he walked home. He fed his cat and lay on his bed until it was night.

Tony knew.

Somehow that was so much worse than God knowing, which of course he did too. Tony's logic was childish, but correct; Michael knew the Lord would forgive him his sin. He was just as sure Tony never would.

When the tentative knock at his door came, Michael was surprised; he hadn't thought they'd be so polite.

When he looked through the peephole, he was shocked to see her standing there.

"Isabella!"

She was in his arms as soon as he opened the door.

"I had to come." She was pale and trembling.

Michael noticed, for the first time, the fine lines around her eyes. He saw the fading bruise on her cheekbone and his heart flooded with sadness and anger.

"You shouldn't be here. It's dangerous; he's probably having you watched."

"No, Michael." Isabella shook her head, smoothing the frown from his forehead with her fingertips. "He can't know. He just suspects. You didn't tell him anything did you?"

"Of course not!"

He closed the door behind her, watching her move into his apartment. It was surreal, her being here, like a dream he'd had many times.

Having grown up surrounded by others, though always a loner, Michael had always longed for a place of his own. He was grateful he'd been allowed his private space here, away from the church. He thought Isabella probably lived in a huge, grand house and, for a moment, he wondered what she thought about his shabby, walk-up studio with its garage-sale furnishings.

Get a grip, he told himself, forgetting all about how grungy his place looked. It looked fine now, with her standing in the middle of it.

She was wearing a soft-looking gray dress that wrapped around her body. It clung to her curves, dipping where she did, hugging her Italian, earth-mother shape. In these days of girls walking around with belly buttons bared and skin-tight clothes that left nothing to the imagination, there was something so much more enticing to Michael about the way Isabella always looked so refined, like a lady.

She bent and slid a finger behind each of her heels, loosening her sandals, and then kicking them off. The deep V of her dress front gaped, and Michael's mouth went dry. It didn't look as if she was wearing anything at all underneath her clothes.

A long time ago, someone had told him sex was like potato chips. If you had it once, you had to have it again and again. Now, he knew they were right; despite all of the reasons he shouldn't, Michael wanted to make love to her.

As if she could see right into him, Isabella slowly untied the bow that held her dress closed over one hip. With a shrug of her shoulders, it slid off her body and—yes, yes, yes—she was naked underneath.

"Even if it only happens this once Michael." She didn't even finish before he was there, his hands scooping up the succulent flesh of her ass, pressing her to him.

He kissed her and moaned. Her mouth was warm and inviting, and made him think immediately of how she'd sucked him in the church. His cock throbbed and jerked with the memory.

She took him by the hand and led him to his bed. She lay down in the middle of it, her hair loose and dark against the stark white of his sheets.

Michael wanted to worship her, to lick every inch of her body, to love her until she wept.

He shed his clothes. He might not have ever done this, but he'd thought about it a million times.

"You're so beautiful," he told her, curling his arm under her head and sweeping a hand over her luscious body.

It was stunning, this feeling of pressing his bare flesh to hers. He'd never once imagined that such a simple thing could feel so good.

Her skin was cool under his palm, but she was hot between her legs. He dipped a finger into her, parting the shallow covering of dark hair there, finding a wet center.

Isabella whimpered, curling her fingers into his hair, pulling him closer.

Michael learned from her. When she spread her thighs and lifted her hips to his touch, he did what he was doing some more. When she frowned or drew back slightly, pressing into his mattress, he shifted and moved from circling his fingers to flicking them until he found just what pleased her.

He kissed her and suckled at her decadent mouth. He tasted her nipples and marveled at the way they transformed from soft smooth flesh to pebbled hardness on his tongue.

He sighed when she turned enough so her hand could slide over his penis. It slicked her palm with its need. He watched, fascinated, as the pupils of her dark eyes dilated with desire.

They moved in slow motion, every caress achingly tender. He touched her with love; he realized he did love her and almost cried right in the middle of it all.

She rolled him over onto his back, and tangled her fingers with his as she straddled him. Her long hair trailed like black silk ribbons over his chest. He closed his eyes, trying to capture the vision of her just like this and keep it forever.

Her body accepted him into her hot, snug depths as if she had always been there, waiting only for him to remember where he belonged. She sheathed him in a velvet grip, rocking back and forth.

It was incredible. This was actually happening, and it was

so much more than he'd ever imagined it could be.

His cock bumped deep inside of her, the tip kissed by something there. She moved against it, nudging him until it felt like her tongue had on the slitted tip of his penis. He shivered, his hands falling to her hips, his fingers gripping, urging her to do it more, faster, harder.

He felt the moment when it changed for her too. Her body grew looser somehow, slicker. Her movements were more fluid. She found a rhythm and curled her toes next to his thighs as she thrust onto him.

He dragged her down, kissing her as they came together silently as if afraid any noise might shatter the pleasure they'd created together. Or maybe they were quiet because they were both scared to death, Michael thought later.

He watched Isabella's smile form and his heart lurched in his chest. There it was, the one thing he'd wanted more than anything—he'd made her smile.

"Come away with me, Bella," he said.

She sat next to him, looking like a young girl suddenly, her hips swathed in his snowy sheets, her hair tumbling around her shoulders. She brushed her fingers over his mouth.

"You know that's impossible, Michael. He'd kill us both."

"Not if we got far enough away. Mexico maybe, some sleepy little town by the sea."

"If this was a movie and we were different people, I'd ask you to kill him. But, it's not." She rose from the bed.

Michael watched her get dressed, slip her shoes on, and put her hair back up into its neat little twist.

He didn't talk anymore. What could he say? She was right.

She sat on the edge of the bed. "I'll think about it, Michael. I promise, and I'll see you soon."

'I love you,' he thought.

"I'll understand if you can't," he lied.

"I love you," she whispered and then she was gone.

Isabella didn't come to church the following Sunday, or the one after that.

Michael realized he didn't even know where she lived. He couldn't think of a way to ask people about her without it seeming odd.

He thought about going to the police and imagined what he'd say: "I'm a priest who fucked the wife of a very bad man and now, I'm worried he's killed her and may be coming after me next." Yeah that'd go over real well.

He could still smell the perfume of their sex on his sheets. Memories of Isabella haunted him. She was an innocent woman lost to a terrible life. She'd reached Michael in ways he'd not even realized until after she was gone. She'd helped him figure himself out. He wanted to repay her, to keep her safe from harm, to love her.

He spent more time in the church, even though it had become the last place he wanted to be, hoping she'd come back.

One day, when he returned from lunch, he found a large white envelope stuffed under his door. Inside, was a one-way plane ticket to Ixtapa, Mexico and a map. On it, a tiny x was circled—an address on the shoreline just south of a town called Barra de Potosi. Nestled in the bottom of the envelope was a familiar strand of black rosary beads.

"You wanted to see me, Michael?" Father Murphy poked his head through the doorway.

Michael's hand shook as he put the envelope down. "Yeah, Father. We need to talk."

"Sure thing, Mike. What's up?"

Robert Murphy liked to think he was "cool" and, in some

ways, he was. Michael had a feeling his coolness wouldn't extend quite this far.

He decided to make it simple. "I screwed up . . . bad. I've got to revoke my vows, quit. I'm sorry, Bob."

"Well, gosh, Michael. Whatever it is can't be that terrible. I know you. You're a good boy. We can work it out, surely. Please talk with me."

Father Murphy looked as confused on the outside as Michael had once felt on the inside. He knew this was the right thing to do and, though he meant it when he'd said he was sorry for what he'd done to the church, his mistake had given him Isabella, and she'd changed his life. The God Michael loved wouldn't condemn him for taking a little long to figure himself out. He'd not expect him to stay either, feeling what he did now.

Michael fingered the edge of the plane ticket on his desk and shook his head. "No, Father Murphy. The only way this can be worked out is if I go, right now."

"This doesn't have anything to do with, uh, boys, does it, Michael?" Murphy's expression was pained.

"No, nothing like that. I promise." Michael put a hand out and shook Father Murphy's when he offered it.

"Why don't you just take a few days off, Mike? Think about it and come see me Sunday. You can't just give up a lifetime's work like this."

"Okay, Father." It was easier to agree than explain.

Michael gathered his few belongings and left. He'd never liked long goodbyes.

The flight to Ixtapa was pleasant. Michael read the Spanish for Gringos booklet from Mexicana Airlines on the way down and learned the important things: *de baño*, *playa*, *no*

mas, *gracias*, *te amo*, and *cerveza*.

He hitched a ride out of town in the back of a beat-up, yellow Ford pick-up.

Driving through the little town of Barra de Potosi, with its colorful covered marketplace and throngs of tourists, Michael managed to forget everything for a while, except the pleasure of being somewhere new.

He smiled, hearing the musical notes a traveling knife-sharpener's whistle made as he wheeled his odd sharpening contraption through the streets. He admired the small girls doing brisk business selling fresh tamales from spotless stainless-steel pails stacked in the baskets of their rusty bicycles.

As the old truck meandered down the scalloped coastline, he saw fishermen pulling their wooden boats onto the beaches and watched several dolphins move quickly through the bay as if they too had somewhere important to get to.

They made it almost all the way to the place where the x marked Michael's map, when the driver—a wizened old man—pulled off at a fork in the road. He pointed at the map and then up one branch of the dusty lane. The message was clear when he tossed Michael's duffle out of the truck-bed.

"*Gracias, amigo*," Michael said.

"*Buena suerte.*"

The house was easy to find. It was the only one at the end of the road, perched high on a cliff overlooking the sea. Even up here, the gusty wind blew sand over Michael's boots, and he could smell the ocean's salted, fresh-fish scent.

Dropping his bag, he rechecked the safety on the snub-nosed .38 he'd bought in Ixtapa before hitching his ride.

Sheer, white curtains billowed through an open window of the inviting house, waving him closer it seemed. An old rocker painted sky blue moved a ghostly to and fro on the porch. Everything else was still. The only sound was the crashing of waves far below.

As Michael started walking again, he prayed Isabella was waiting.

TRICKED

The first time I saw her in the flesh, I knew she'd be trouble. But trouble is my business, so I didn't worry until later.

I'd driven in from the City of Angels, losing myself in a long stretch of desert nothingness, finding it again in the bright neon sunburst that is Las Vegas.

I knew just where to look for her—as far on the wrong side of the tracks as one could get in Sin City. In my line of work, it pays to be cozy with bad people and worse places. I had pictures, so spotting her wasn't difficult.

I'd thought this would be a routine job. In and out, done. A dog, a steak, and a hefty paycheck waited for me at home.

Then I saw her, Sky Harlow, and I wasn't so sure I'd called this one right at all.

She wasn't what I'd expected. Say chippy from sleeze-ville Vegas, and you didn't picture this Snow White, Goth princess, siren-witch. She belonged on the screen or in a painting, not walking the boulevard. The girl in the pictures I'd seen was younger, fresh-scrubbed, but I could still see her under the makeup. Smoke and mirrors was her game, just like mine. Like always recognizes like.

I rolled my window down. She leaned in, all femme fatale, kitten-with-a-whip gorgeous, and agreed to come with me to a cheap motel off-strip. Five hundred bills had more to do with her trust than my good looks.

I sat in the room's only chair, careful not to touch the armrests. The place reeked of stale smoke and paid-for sex. Outside, I heard loud voices, car horns, and the screech of tires. I focused on her. It wasn't hard to do. Sky was a vision of succulent flesh on display. A lock of hair fell like a raven's wing over her left eye whenever she looked down—innocence defiled, and liking it.

She perched on the edge of the bed, her knees almost touching mine. I drew away and, spreading her legs, she showed me that she wore nothing beneath her slinky red skirt. Her cunt was smooth and had a tender pink center. Nothing I'd not seen before.

"Please, don't do that." My hands cupped her knees, pushing them together. Her skin was hot and I pulled away as if burned. Maybe I was in hell. I was dizzy.

"Then get talking, Mister. I haven't got all night."

She crossed her arms over pert little breasts. They spilled fetchingly over tight black leather—a corset that hugged her tiny waist like a lover's hands. She really wasn't my type. I liked my women tall, cool, and blonde. Classy. Sky was raw sex, blood and razors, stings and nettles with an angel's face.

"I want you to talk. I want to know about you, about your life." I wasn't lying. I'd been paid to find out, but looking at her, I really wanted to know who the fuck she was. I cared and had no idea why.

"What're you? Some kind of reporter?" Her eyes narrowed into black-rimmed, violet slits—cat's eyes, hoyden's eyes, liar's eyes.

"I'm just someone with cash enough to indulge a healthy curiosity. What more do you need to know?" I made my tone harder—bullets on brick. It worked.

"All right, so what do you want to talk about?" Her voice went soft as butter melting.

She pulled her jacket around her even though it had to be pushing eighty in the close room. Her small movements produced the scent of her perfume—flowery—poppies and opium. I inhaled it like a drug, and that's when I knew I was in deep shit.

"Tell me about the men you sleep with."

She laughed. "We don't do a lot of sleeping, Mister."

"All right, tell me about the men you fuck."

"Well, I don't always fuck them. Sometimes they want me to suck them or just watch them jerk off. Maybe show them my tits or talk dirty to them. Do you like that, Mister?"

"Do you like it?"

"Sometimes." She looked me right in the eye. I liked that.

She frowned, and I could see her youth in the expression. She had a dimple in her chin, and baby-fat still clung to her cheeks. The rest of her body was all woman, the stuff of every bad boy's wet dreams, but scrub away the makeup and she was little more than a child. Old enough that the law usually didn't hassle her—she'd assured me of that in the car on the way here. She didn't tell me, but I knew she was twenty-five, not much younger than me.

"Tell me about the times you like." My cock was rock hard, and I crossed my legs to hide it.

She leaned forward, her tongue taking a slow trip along the curves of her upper lip—pink on slut-red glitter. "Well, I have one regular who's very handsome, very clean. He always talks to me first, almost like you're doing, and then he watches me masturbate."

"Do people ask for that often?" I imagined her spread out, fingers buried in her pussy, and almost came in my pants.

"Sometimes." Her voice went stainless steel cold.

"Don't worry. I'm not judging you."

She smiled, coy and coquettish, but wary. "I'm not worried. You paid me, so it's your dime. But, it's pretty fucking strange you giving me five hundred bucks just to sit here and talk. You want me to talk nasty to you? Is that it? You want to hear what bad girls like?"

I ignored her questions mainly because the answer was yes, but I had a job to do. "Don't other clients sometimes have odd requests, ask you to do things you don't understand?"

"Of course." She leaned back into the pillows, curling onto her side to face me.

She seemed more relaxed, and I let her talk. Let most people talk, and they'll get around to telling you what you want to know, you won't even have to ask.

"Weirdest one was a guy who wanted me to suck him off while he sang "Danny Boy". He was Irish. Cried when he was done. I didn't ask for the story. He was in enough pain."

Her voice was girlish now, soft, and sweet. This girl was a chameleon. All she needed was an idea of what a customer wanted, and she became it. She couldn't quite get a handle on me though, which was the way I wanted it.

"How much did you charge for that?" I imagined her in a dirty room similar to this one, on her knees in front of some old Irishman, and wanted to slap her, and then fuck her silly. Hell, I'd even sing.

What the fuck was wrong with me? This was a job, nothing more to either of us. She wasn't a hooker with a heart of gold, and I wasn't the tough but kind private eye. This was no movie. It was life— rough and real and vicious as a pit-bull in a room full of kitty cats.

Her matter-of-fact voice brought me back. "I did it for fifty. With no fucking, I didn't even have to clean up after." Her heels snagged the bumpy orange bedspread as she sat up again, shrugging her shoulders.

"And, did you like doing that?" I really wanted to know.

"Not especially. But, in a way, I was helping him. He needed me. And I needed the money, so it's all good." She shrugged her shoulders and drew her knees to her chest. I saw a flash of bare ass before she remembered my instructions and smoothed her skirt down, pretty legs dangling over the edge of the bed.

The image of her naked curves burned a hole in my memory. I kept flashing on it, and my palms itched. I wanted to touch that perfect white skin. Instead, I lit a cigarette.

I managed a smoke ring, though I was beginning to feel slightly buzzed and was fighting a growing urge to get up, walk out, and end this now. I found a loose thread on my cuff and worried it with my fingernail.

"Does your pimp make you earn a certain amount every night?"

"I don't have a pimp. I stay away from the popular places, and no one messes with me." She cocked her dimpled chin at me, purple eyes flashing. Proud and pissed off, a dangerous combination, one that made my heart and cock throb in unison.

"How'd you decide to make this your profession?"

"I didn't decide. Life did."

"Tell me about it. Don't you have friends, a family? How about a boyfriend?" I stubbed out my cigarette.

"I don't have or need anyone, Mister, and the last person I told my life story to said it was, what was the word, oh yeah, predictable." She smiled a brittle smile, her eyes sharp as nails. "Now, you've about used up your five hundred and that doesn't even come close to covering this kind of soul-searching shit anyway."

I almost felt bad enough to stop, but not quite.

"Are you happy? Sexually?" I was willing to play by her rules, to have more time with her. I was going to need it.

"I don't see what I do for a living as having anything to do with my own sexual happiness if that's what you mean. The two are separate, business and pleasure."

"You mean it's never good for you?"

"Well, it's not all bad. Like I said, some of my clients are very nice." She stood up on platform shoes —wet looking, black leather with stiletto sharp heels.

I stood too. I was unsettled, antsy. I stepped closer so she wouldn't see that my dick was a pole down my leg. I felt her warmth, breathed it in, and drowned in the violet pools of her eyes.

"Tell me how it is, fucking so many men in one day."

She arched her back, her nipples kissing my shirtfront— leather on linen. Her breath was sweet, her tone naughty. "I love it."

That was it. I slammed into her, knocking her back against the door with a thud, my hand jammed between her legs. She was wet and my fingers slipped easily through her folds as her leg lifted and curved around my waist. I jerked her head back; handfuls of black hair filled my fist.

"I love this," she said, sliding my zipper down, taking my dick in her hands and rocking into me, her fingers hot and slithery, just like the rest of her.

"You love the business, huh?" I groaned as she jacked me off, my thumb and forefinger catching her clit and giving it a twist. I shifted to give her better access to my raging prick.

"You didn't pay for sex, Mister. You paid to talk." She leaned forward and kissed my jaw, right where I could feel a tick of tension throbbing. It calmed, but the rest of me remained taut, coiled, and agitated.

I cupped her cunt and the swell of it wet my fingers. They slipped up inside her. I held her, just like that—pinned to the door, impaled on my hand, my nose touching hers.

"So, this is pleasure?" I breathed in the scent of her—

pussy and honey, bee-stung flowers and nitro.

"Yes."

She didn't beat around the bush. I liked that. My cock liked it too. It oozed a pearl-sized droplet of pre-cum. She smoothed it over my glans, swirling her palm, making it wet too.

I spread her wide with my thumbs, cock poised at her pink gate. Then I remembered. She was a whore, and I didn't have a condom. Fuck.

She laughed and reached into her corset top, pulling out a foil packet. "This the problem, Mister?"

She tore the packet open with her teeth and, with expert fingers, rolled the latex sheath over my cock, winking as she snapped the tight ring at the base. It stung. I liked that too.

"Now, fuck me. Fuck me hard, fuck me fast and shut the fuck up."

I did it. I slammed into her, wanting to hurt her, and love her, and somehow make her remember me as something more than a cock. I stopped asking myself why and just went with it, sinking into her over and over again, reaching down to fiddle with her clit until she writhed and moaned, and became just a girl, just a girl who wanted what I was giving her.

I didn't say another word. I was quiet, purposeful, hard like she wanted it—hard as concrete, hard as my heart, hard as her life. I fucked her. She fucked me. It wasn't pretty, or romantic. It wasn't the sort of thing you see in movies or read about in books. It was real.

We almost fell as we came, shattered and clinging, panting and grunting. My knees shook. I laid my head against the door, tucking it next to hers, and closed my eyes.

Jesus fucking Christ. This girl knew what I needed and somehow, in the middle of it all, I knew what she needed too. I lifted her from the floor and let her wind herself around me. I held her, and soothed her, petted her and kissed her. I loved her.

When it was all over, she gently unrolled the filled condom—tossing it in the trash—zipped up my pants and smoothed down her skirt. Her hair had fallen away from her forehead, and those huge violet eyes looked right into mine as she reached around to finger the gun I had strapped to my side.

"So, you going to tell me the real deal about why you came here and just who the fuck you are?"

It was like ice water in my face, her tone, her look. It was true; I'd come to do a job, but somehow I'd gotten here, to a place where the job didn't matter anymore for the first time in my sorry life. Sometime between the money changing hands and cumming, I'd seen inside this girl, and didn't want to hurt her. Trouble was somebody else did, somebody a lot meaner than me. I couldn't tell her that though, no fucking way.

So, I shook my head and took her hand from my gun, kissing her fingers as she wrapped them around mine. "No can do, Sky. Just believe me when I tell you: that meant something to me."

She jerked the door open before I could say anything else. "Fuck you and your something, Mister."

She walked away, hips rolling, her finger forming the universal punctuation to her statement.

She didn't even look back.

I didn't make it home. The dog went hungry, and the steak rotted in my fridge.

I checked into one of the fancy hotels on the strip. I poured myself a whiskey, spilling some on my trousers. My hands were shaking. Once upon a time, I'd have ordered an expensive call girl for the night, to ease my tensions, but tonight I sat alone.

I drank unseen behind a wall of glass. Garish lights in rainbow colors flashed up and down the street as I thought about my newest problem—Sky.

I rummaged in my bag, pulling out the letters and pictures, putting everything else in the file aside.

The first letter was yellow with age, handwritten in an old woman's shaky hand.

Dear Dr. Jonathan Soames,

My girl Tashia bore you a child. I tried, but had to give her up. She got eyes like yours. It's my time and I thought you should know. You all she got now.

Iris Hughes

Sky's grandmother had tried to do the right thing, letting Dr. Soames know about his illegitimate offspring. Probably just heard Doctor and pictured Marcus-fucking-Welby. I guessed Sky's mom hadn't wanted her mama to know the truth, about her life or her sugar daddy.

The second letter was a couple of months old, on fancy letterhead, the kind of stuff I couldn't afford.

Dear Dr. Soames,

I've enclosed the full report on your daughter. As we discussed on the phone, she supports herself by prostitution. She goes by the name Sky Harlow and works the strip in Las Vegas by the Suncoast Motel. I've enclosed pictures and directions. Her mother, Tashia Hughes, died shortly after giving birth to her (see the enclosed death certificate and burial information). As far as I have been able to trace, you are Sky's only living relative. I wish you luck, whatever you decide to do.

Godspeed,
Dick Jones, PI

I knew Dick. He was a straight-up shamus. He'd done his part, cashed his paycheck, and probably forgotten all about the good Doctor and his hooker daughter.

As for me, well, I didn't have any paper trail. Guys like me never do. That's why the Doc ended up in my office. Offered me $2,500 to find out who'd miss Sky when she was gone and a lot more to tie up all the loose ends.

Now I worried about what would happen when I got back to LA, about the next hatchet man the Doc would hire to do the job if I only dropped the dime on her for the change. How they'd do it. When.

I worried over Sky and why not? Nobody else would, not even the cops, not that types like us would ever knock on their door.

But, what could I do?

I'd done some checking and knew the Doc had an heiress wife and twin girls almost the same age as Sky. He had a Bel Air mansion, memberships to country clubs; he golfed with the Mayor and lunched with the famous. He had a lot to protect.

I imagined what would happen if I came back empty-handed. What would happen to me and to Sky? I spun different yarns in my head, trying them on for size, all night long. The endings were mostly the same—dead people, sorry people.

I thought about going to Sky, spilling it all to her. Would it be better for her if she knew the score, knew what was coming? Would she hate me? Could we make a clean sneak? Would she want to?

I was tired. I slept when the sun rose.

Late the next day I drove down that long, flashy strip, watching floods of humanity mingle in the heat and insanity that is Las Vegas. Some smiled, some looked pissed off. Other than the shimmering lights, gaudy in the bright daylight, it could have been anywhere. Same faces. Same shit. Different day.

Most days, I do what I do because every day does bring something new—a new set of problems, a new puzzle, a new reason to exist. Every time my door opens, it's an adventure. Sometimes it's as simple as helping an old lady catch the neighbor trying to poison her cat, sometimes it's a lot more complicated.

This was one of those times.

I came to that place at the end of Las Vegas Boulevard, where the lights fade to desert emptiness and the street splits—left to the City of Angels on-ramp, right to the bad side of town.

I'd thought it over all night and, in the end, turned down the only road I could.

HOW JACKSON CRUMB
REMEMBERED HOW TO LIVE

This is the story of how Jackson Crumb remembered how to live.

It all began on a Tuesday. Every previous Tuesday, during Jack's ten years at Hartford Life Insurance, had been the same—up at 6:00, showered and fed (one cup exactly of oatmeal with a side of seasonal fruit) by 7:00. Out the door by 7:10.

Jack Crumb firmly believed in routine. At the office, the first order of business each Tuesday was the attorney's review of claims pending lawsuits. As head of claims, Jack chaired the meeting and considered the duty to be one of the shining points in his usually unshiny life. Here, he ruled.

This Tuesday, things took an unusual turn when, in the middle of what had been a very uneventful, normal risk management meeting, a new advocacy attorney stood to argue a case. She represented the client though, technically, she worked for Hartford Life.

Usually, Jack paid scant attention to whatever the lawyers had to say, having already decided before entering the conference room which cases he would settle and which ones he would fight. Nothing any attorney had to say would change his mind.

This case, and this attorney, were different.

Her voice was what first caught his attention. She waited for silence, which in itself was unusual. Most of them just barged in, said what they had to say and fled, as if knowing it would make no difference anyway and just wanting to get the whole thing over with.

She was from the south. Her name was Jolene Fisher. Jack thought that perhaps she had taken elocution lessons, for her drawl was subtle, drawing out her vowels and adding flavor to her husky voice. Jack sat up straighter in his chair, taking in her fresh, earnest face as he listened to her plea for the client, one Spinner Shydler.

"As you know, the estate of Mr. Shydler is suing Hartford Life for non-payment of the claim."

"The man killed himself. What didn't they understand about the policy's suicide clause, Ms. Fisher?" This from Betty Harrington, the only woman on the risk committee.

"They are prepared to argue that Mr. Shydler's death was accidental and, after reviewing their attorney's brief, I've come to the conclusion that they have a case. It is my recommmendation that we pay out the million rather than risk an almost certain loss in court, ending up having to pay damages plus fees."

Jack flipped through Jolene's report, the coroner's, and the adjuster's who'd rejected the claim. Seemed clear enough. Shydler—a rock musician of apparently some note—had strung himself up from a beam over the whirlpool tub in his Hotel Metro suite and met his maker. End of story. The only witness was a doped up groupie who had managed to tell the cops that he'd done it himself and had died while she watched, helpless to save him.

"What's the gist of their argument, Ms. Fisher?"

"They claim the death was accidental and are prepared to prove it, showing the deceased had no intention of killing himself."

"How, exactly, do they intend to convince a jury that he hanged himself accidentally?" As cute as she was, Jackson wasn't going to cut her any slack.

"They are going to claim Mr. Shydler was into erotic asphyxiation. You know, where someone intentionally cuts off oxygen to their brain during sexual stimulation? Remember when kids were dying all over playing that choking game? Same thing, only a grown-up version. It is the major cause of accidental hangings worldwide and the reason why his attorneys might well kick our asses in court. Unless we can prove the man intended to kill himself, we're going to lose." She was all riled up, her eyes flashing, and her fingers gripping her pink leather portfolio. For the first time in a very long time, Jackson felt two things— the desire to change his mind during a risk management meeting and a yearning to ask a woman out on a date.

As a single man, living in Chicago, he'd done the singles-bar scene, the meet-and-mingle parties, and the blind dates, but hadn't met anyone even close to being Ms. Right. Anything more than casual, mutually agreed upon, sex with someone he wasn't crazy in love with seemed rather messy. Jack hated messes. He fancied his relatives and friends discussed his singleness when he was not around and labeled him an enigma.

"They'll do no such thing, Ms. Fisher. Anyone who puts a belt around their neck and jumps off a whirlpool surely knows death is possible. Claim rejected!" Betty Harrington said, decisively.

Before things got too out of hand, and everyone forgot just who ran things around here, Jack said, firmly, "The higher-ups have taken a keen interest in this case and, obviously, wish to avoid a media circus. The sooner we hand down our decision, the better. In the interest of time, Betty, you review the coroner's statement and shoot me a memo before you leave tonight. Jeff, you take the adjuster's statement and do the same. Ms. Fisher, you and I will work through lunch reviewing Mr. Shydler's lawyer's supporting documents. We'll hand down our decision in the morning."

"I am so glad you didn't just rule with Ms. Harrington. I'd heard you were a hard-ass, but just knew someone in your position had to be able to see both sides." Jolene said, hurrying to keep up with him as they left the conference room.

Jack let the hard-ass comment slide as her compliment filled him with pleasure. He was not here to make friends and knew being in his position meant garnering naysayers. It was a small price to pay for power.

"Your argument was compelling, Ms. Fisher. I may be a hard-ass, but I'm no idiot," he winked at her, and they both chuckled. A warm glow ignited within Jack's chest.

"I was thinking we could order in? Maybe just get some of those sandwiches they always have in the boardroom on Tuesdays? We'd get a lot more done in your office. Is that okay with you?" She was so cute, clutching that pink portfolio, her eyes shining with the light of good intentions and hard work.

"Great idea."

They took the elevator up to Jack's top floor office. He saw the glances his co-workers gave him as he strolled past with the delectable Ms. Fisher and felt a swelling of pride. She really was a sweet looking thing, all legs and curves and flaming red hair. The freckles made it cute and not whorish. The girl was a southern bit of fluff in her cream Chanel knockoff with the pink piping. Every man he worked with looked at him with envy and Jack congratulated himself on his decision to take her up to his office. He would show her where she was wrong and convince her to change her mind about the case. Blown away by his commanding confidence and his mental prowess, she would agree to have lunch again sometime, maybe even drinks or coffee.

"Bring us some sandwiches," he told his secretary.

His office had huge windows, potted plants, and Kandinsky prints. The chairs opposite his desk were intentionally small. He started around to his own large, leather chair, but Ms. Fisher settled on his couch, littering his coffee table with folders and looking at him expectantly.

"Ms. Fisher—" he started.

"Please, would you call me Jolene? Ms. Fisher is my mom!" She smiled at him with such feckless charm that he nodded and sat next to her as if they were in a living room, not a business office.

Jack felt dizzy, light-headed. He forgot what he'd intended to say when his wool-covered knee bumped into Jolene's nylon clad one.

"Jolene. Yes, of course. Pretty name."

"Why, thank you! My mama was a Dolly fan."

She fluttered her lashes over sky-blue eyes, and Jack's cock twitched. This really was turning out to be an unusual day.

"Sandwiches!" his secretary announced, coming into his office carrying a tray loaded with turkeys on wheat and bottled waters.

Jack jumped, like a boy caught with his hands in the babysitter's panties. Jolene giggled. Jack's secretary, a consummate professional, pretended not to notice anything odd, and after setting out the lunch on the coffee table, she left. The door closed behind her with a soft click.

Jack casually ran his fingers through his bristly crew cut and wasn't surprised to find his forehead damp. Jolene was really getting to him. Get a grip, he told himself. You are a grown man just sitting next to a pretty girl on a couch.

"Please tell me Ms. . . . . Jolene, what evidence will Mr. Shydler's lawyers present?"

He sipped water, watching her tuck into the sandwiches as if she hadn't eaten in a week. He found her hearty appetite oddly appealing, especially enjoying it when she flicked her pink tongue out to catch crumbs perched on the pillow of her lush bottom lip. He had a difficult time concentrating on her answer, but was attentive when she said, "He liked his sex kinky, Mr. Crumb and that's something a lot of jurors will relate to."

"Oh? Do you think most people like kinky sex, Jolene?"

"I know they do!" She laughed, and her cheeks turned pink. "I mean, most people might not admit it, but who doesn't like sex, really? And, once you start in a kinky direction, well, it's hard to get back on the missionary road. Anyone who's ever tried that sort of thing could tell you that."

"That's what Mr. Shydler's team will argue? That he drove off into the wilds of kinky sex and ended up with a noose around his neck? You think a jury will relate to that kind of extreme?" Jack wanted to ask her what sort of sex she liked, but really, that would be about the most unprofessional thing he could think of to discuss during a business meeting.

Her skirt had ridden up her slinky thighs. He swallowed, lifting his gaze to hers and keeping it there with effort.

"Absolutely! They have the witness to swear that's what he was up to. She was jacking him off when he slipped! Excuse my language. The girl is an eyewitness and is only one of a parade of women who are willing to testify to the sort of sex games Spinner Shydler liked to play. Apparently he was into everything." She waggled an eyebrow at him and grinned that gamine grin.

He had to cross his legs. His dick was throbbing madly.

All this sex talk, knee brushing, and lip licking was making him long to shove Jolene back on the couch and yank that Suzy-creampuff skirt of hers up to see if she was wearing panties. He cleared his throat and tried to look pensive as if he was considering her words and not wondering what color her panties might be, or if her pussy was smooth or furry. Was she a thong girl or hipster one? He imagined her in white cotton panties and had to close his eyes to collect himself.

"He was into everything?" He couldn't help himself from asking.

"Everything." She flipped open a file folder and pointed at bulleted items on a page. "Erotic asphyxiation was just the start. He also got off on algolagnia, andromimetophilia, aquaphilia, and agalmatophilia and those are just the A's!"

"Do you know what all those things are?" He figured the aqua one had something to do with water.

"I looked them up!" She beamed at him and crossed her legs. Jack caught a whiff of flowery perfume and leaned closer, like a bee drawn to a honey pot.

"Aren't you the industrious one?"

"I think knowledge is important," she said, with a crisp little nod of her head. The motion set her soft curls to bouncing and once more Jackson was distracted as a tendril of red hair curled itself lovingly around one of her full, silk-bloused breasts.

"Yes. Yes, indeed." Jack said, kicking himself mentally for sounding so inane.

"So, do you see now why I said we just need to settle this one to avoid having our asses handed to us on a very expensive, very public platter?"

She had a nice ass. He'd noticed it when they'd entered his office. He'd been talking to his secretary, and Jolene had walked ahead of him. He liked her shoes too, sensible pumps made frisky by the pink leather. She dangled one from her foot, and it dropped to his carpet as she wiggled her toes, each little piggy shiny with fuchsia polish.

"What?" He shook his head, dizzy again, dragging his eyes from her feet to her face.

"I was afraid of this, Mr. Crumb. Not that I agree with what they say about you being a hard-ass who always makes his decisions before even looking at the evidence. Our meeting today has shown me that is so not true. But, this is a difficult case to settle, I know that. I mean, on the one hand, it seems so cut and dried, but on the other, I really do think it was an accident and just not worth fighting over." She sighed, flopping back on the couch, wearing a defeated scowl.

"No. I mean, yes. I agree. It's just I am not convinced that a jury will not simply see the facts. He hung himself. Period. Even with the list of weird sex stuff, where's the proof he didn't do it on purpose?" He fought the urge to take her in his arms and soothe her even as he argued. He wondered if she liked foot rubs.

"I think his lawyers will play up the fantasy life he had and work the happily ever after angle. They'll show he had a history of living it up, even when it came to sex. This wasn't a man who was depressed. He went out in the middle of a kinky drunken hand job for goodness sakes! They had room service on the way too. Cristal and porterhouses. I checked."

"Nice!"

"The hand job or the steaks?" She giggled and scooted closer to him.

"Both!" Jackson felt something break free in his chest as he laughed with her, flinging off his usual guarded demeanor and saying exactly what he was thinking for once.

"See? I think the jury will feel that way too. They will totally understand why the guy was turned on and happy and not even close to killing himself!" The strength of her convictions or his air conditioning had made her nipples hard, and it was all Jack could do not to pinch one of them, just to see whether she would melt, moan, or wiggle in response.

I love hand jobs, he wanted to say. "You've convinced me. Just one thing. What's a happily ever after angle?" he asked, instead.

"It's like in Disney movies, where the girl is all la-la-la in the forest, animals dancing around, bees singing, flowers blooming and all? What always happens? She meets the prince, he takes her to places she has never been before, and she loves it, right? And, just when you think they are going to live happily ever after, something awful happens and you see how she could have lived even more fully when she had the chance. The only thing is, in a fairy tale the girl always gets that second chance and goes on to live happily ever after. Poor Spinner won't get to. Cue the violins." She pushed out her lower lip fetchingly, made doe eyes at him, and that was pretty much that. Jackson's life changed forever.

"Do you believe in happily ever after, Jolene?" His fingertip brushed the side of her hand where it rested on the couch next to his thigh.

"Of course I do, Jack. I'm from the south," she said, as if that made a lick of sense.

"Would you go out to dinner with me tonight?" he asked as she slid her hand over his.

"Can I give you a hand job on the way home?"

Jackson laughed, sliding his hand under her gorgeous hair, cupping the nape of her neck. "Absolutely. You wearing panties?"

Years later, telling the story to their grandkids, Jolene always left out the kinky sex talk and just spoke of Granddad's confidence, his brains, and the way he'd swept her right out of her pink pumps that day in his office. Jackson just made sure everyone knew that without Jolene, he would never have realized he'd been barely living until she rescued him from his very dull, very pompous self.

WHITER THAN SNOW

Katie stood on the front steps of the church. Looking up at Gothic gargoyles, stone angels, and soaring windows, she shivered.

Her friend Johnny hadn't lied; Saint de Sade's was amazing.

She held the heavy door open for a remarkably authentic-looking group of fresh-faced girls dressed in nun's habits and walked inside.

The door closed behind her with a dull thud, and she hesitated in the cavernous entry hall, her eyes adjusting to the dimly lit space, her heart pounding.

And they left the church, free of fear and ecstasy possessed, and they suffered no more for they were filled with awe, a sign hanging on the wall read.

Katie was trying to recall the last time she had been free of fear, ecstasy possessed or filled with awe when a young man wearing flowing robes appeared from the shadows.

"Katie O'Malley?"

She jumped, startled. "Yes?"

"You're late. Come with me."

She followed him, walking into a chapel filled with old air, hushed whispers, and candlelight. Stained glass windows, lit by the dying sun, glowed with rainbow hues. Neat rows of polished pews flanked a crimson path.

The confessional waited down front—a wooden, closet-like box with two doors.

Katie shivered, rivers of excitement gripping her belly with greedy fingers. She was giddy, nervous and, for one anxiety-ridden moment, she wondered if this experience would be more than she can handle.

"Close the door behind you, and latch it," her escort said, holding the confessional door open.

She wondered why there was a latch at all as she obediently stepped inside and fit the bar into its loop. Was it there to keep people out or to keep her in should she change her mind and decide to run—not enough to stop her but enough to slow her down? She forced this alarming thought out of her mind, surrendering instead to her almost overwhelming thirst for the things she'd come here for. For years, she had tried to leave her sins in the past, but still they lurked like monsters in her closets. This was the only thing she had not tried, the only thing she thought might work.

Inside the confessional, it was shadowy and quiet. She pulled the kneeler down, wincing as her knees settled onto the hard, uncushioned wood. No comfort for the sinners at Saint de Sade's.

She heard footsteps, then a door opening and closing with a squeak. She held her breath and peered through the screen dividing the confessional, her gaze searching, her ears pricking with sounds heard—rustling clothing, a breath taken and let go.

"Hello, my child. I will hear your confession. Out of thine own mouth will I judge thee."

Jesus, this was intense. Johnny had told her what to expect, but the combination of her profane desires and the stark reality of this place shook her. Saint de Sade's prided itself on offering only the most authentic experience; it said so right on their website.

She wondered, in the moment it took her to answer, about the priest. Why had he decided to serve in this way? How had he reconciled things she could not, both within herself and with the teachings of the church she had long ago abandoned? Her organized mind searched for order, in what was rapidly sliding into the surreal, and could find none.

"Bless me, Father, for I have sinned," she began in a rush.

Pushing her thoughts away, prompted by the priest's opening words, her own came easier than expected. "It's been a long time since my last confession," she said, rather than admitting she could not even remember the last time she'd been in any kind of church.

She confessed. Some things were very hard to tell him, but she did; it was why she'd come. She told him everything, all the secret things she had held onto all this time. As the monsters came out of her closets, she began to cry.

He listened, silent, apparently unmoved by her tears or her crimes.

The heavy aura of her confessed sins surrounding her, Katie wiped away her tears, feeling an odd mixture of shame, fear, and relief.

"That's all. Everything," she said, her breath hitching. "Can you help me?"

She'd intended to confess it all, and had managed to get out even the most agonizing things, but worried maybe she'd lied even to herself—justifying some sins, forgetting others. As she waited for the priest to decide her fate, she wondered if the price of atonement would be more than she could bear or the necessary punishment more than he could offer. Maybe her sins were too great to be forgiven.

It suddenly felt intensely sexual to her—her confession offered for the priest's empathy, the give and take bleeding together. The agony of her want was tinged with exquisitely painful guilt. Being penetrated this way was a passionate, rending mind-fuck—without fingers, tongue, or cock—and she longed for more.

"You have suffered greatly wearing the yoke of your wrongdoings. I can help you cast it off only if you truly wish to be free of its weight, and do exactly as I tell you. Stand up. Come close," the priest said, his voice nearer as Katie obeyed.

Her knees quivered as she pressed her cheek to the latticed wall of the confessional. She thought she could feel his warmth on the other side, and closed her eyes. This was what she wanted—something real, something she could feel in a way she understood.

There was a nickering of wood sliding over wood and a sudden stirring of air as he opened the old-fashioned screen partition, exposing her from breast to thigh. "Wash me, and I shall be whiter than snow. Sprinkle me with cleansing blood and I shall be clean again and, after you have punished me, give me back my joy again. So sayeth the Lord."

The words sparked a frantic flutter in Katie's heart as the priest slid his hand between her thighs and squeezed her pussy, his thumb exploring through her skirt and panties. She whimpered, frozen in place. Pangs of fear clashed with her excitement as the priest spoke of blood and fondled her.

This was already so much more than she'd anticipated, though exactly what she needed.

"Did you know blood in the moonlight glitters, black?" The priest asked the question in his now familiar, soothing tone.

She didn't, but she pictured it now and moaned, her thoughts a disorganized jumble splashed with ebony, blood-soaked images. "No, I didn't know that."

"Exit the confessional, and go through the open door behind it. It will close, and you will kneel there and wait."

Fumbling with the latch, Katie bolted from the confessional avoiding the eyes of those in line. She was very aware of the red flush on her cheeks and the obvious press of her hardened nipples against her shirt. She prayed there wasn't a visible wet spot on the front of her skirt and, looking down, was mortified to discover a dark smudge.

She walked through the doorway and kneeled as instructed, one hand curled protectively over the damp circle on her skirt. Waiting, her knees touched the ground, but the rest of her seemed to fly away, separate, with no anchor, no salvation. Dizzy, she spread her fingers on the cold stone floor for support.

She wondered if there was mercy to be had and if she would want it. Would she rather keep this burning need inside or give it to the priest? She decided she wouldn't want benevolence, even as apprehension blossomed in her belly, her imagination rampant with dark fantasies of the punishment she'd come for—feared as much as longed for.

She craved an elusive savior, who would not be swayed, who would know what she needed. The stained glass windows overhead and the sweetly drifting choral music would not make this one soft. He would do what needed to be done.

Never before had Katie felt so close to what religion had promised but not delivered—as she hath done, so shall it be done to her; eye for eye, tooth for tooth. Until she felt it, the monsters in her closets would haunt her.

She fidgeted, wondering how long she would have to wait. The thought of kneeling in the open for a long time, alone except for the occasional passerby, mortified her. She imagined rising and running out the doors of the church. Home. Safe. The thought made her giddy and ashamed, all at once.

She didn't rise, and the priest came to where she knelt, her eyes cast downward.

He lifted her chin, his fingers curling warm and intimately beneath until their gazes met.

He was younger than Katie had expected. He wore his dark hair long, held back in a neat ponytail. His black shirt was fitted with a crisp, collared band of white.

Once more, she rode the edge between anxiety and pleasure. Everything about the priest was as expected and yet shocking all the same.

"Clasp your hands behind your neck." His assured, gentle tone compelled her to lift her trembling fingers, linking them behind her head.

"Lovely." The priest's fingers circled her throat. His thumbs pressed for a dizzying moment to the hollow between the curves of her collarbones.

He leaned closer, close enough for a kiss. "Here the wicked cease from troubling, and the weary are at rest." His lips captured her gasp with one tiny suckle of her bottom lip.

"Remove your shirt." His whisper was warm on her cheek.

The shock of his words hit her like a slap, causing goose bumps and a thrill of pleasure mingled with anxiety. She shed her snug t-shirt, folding it neatly, pushing it against the wall.

His gaze dropped to her bare breasts, and she fought an urge to cover herself with shielding, cupped hands. She felt bare, vulnerable in body and spirit.

Her fingers gripped her knees as he clasped a collar around her throat. It was black leather—not too loose, not too tight, but just right. The smell was sharp and distinctive. A ring hung from the front and the priest lifted it, dangling it from his fingers before attaching a leash. Metal rasped closed against metal, everything made momentous by the lack of discussion, by the surety of the collaring and leashing, the quick efficiency, and matter-of-factness of it.

"The Lord gave and the Lord hath taken away. Blessed be the name of the Lord."

Katie could not move. She could not speak, and her thoughts halted; what he'd done was so humbling it stilled her inside and out. At last, she thought, someone who understands.

He gazed at her—collared, leashed, kneeling—and, in the silence between them she felt acceptance and recognition. Aching need hung in the air like a live presence.

"Come." He wrapped the leather handle of the leash around his fist. Silver links trailed through his fingers. He didn't look back as he walked away, leaving Katie to scramble to her feet and follow or be dragged behind.

They walked down the winding hall until he stopped before a door Katie hadn't noticed, its wood worn to a hue the same shade as the stone lining the passage. The priest opened the door, revealing a cave-like alcove. On one wall hung a variety of crops, floggers, whips, canes, belts and paddles. There was even a ruler, long and wickedly thin. Looking at it, her insides quaked, and she fought memories of unjust childhood punishments and evil nuns. Unable to look at the ruler, she turned away and watched the priest loop her leash over a chair and reach for a pair of black gloves resting on a low table. He picked them up and tugged them onto his hands, fingers wiggling into snug leather.

In the priest's gaze were compassion and understanding. As if reading her mind, he said, "Let not the sun go down upon your sins, for every man shall bear his own burden and pay his own price."

Katie shivered, nodding, wanting desperately to let go of her anger, her guilt and her monsters.

"Pick," he said, tilting his head toward the display.

With butterflies in her stomach, she looked back at the

whips, paddles, and other instruments of punishment and reached, with only the slightest hesitation, for the thing that had caught her attention from the first moment she'd seen it, a thin black riding whip. She lifted it from the wall, holding it out to the priest as she knelt again, offering herself in the gesture he had not asked for.

"How can you do what needs to be done, Father?" she finally asked him, trembling as her gaze searched his.

"If any man is a bearer of the word and not a doer, he is like a man beholding his face in a glass; if he beholds himself and turns away, he forgets what manner of man he is," he said, taking the whip from her. Sliding a petting palm over the curve of her head, he allowed her to nuzzle her cheek into his leather-covered fingers.

"Good girl," he said, the praise penetrating Katie, his approval felt as contentment, knowing she had pleased him by kneeling, even if she still questioned.

He turned and dipped his fingers into a basin, sprinkling droplets of holy water onto the whip, blessing it. She knew this without him saying it.

"It will sting more wet," he said before saying the words that made it final. "*In nomine Patris, et Filii, et Spiritus Sancti. Amen.*"

He helped Katie to her feet and led her back into the hall, tugging the leash sharply when she paused, forcing her into a brisker stride until they came to another door. It creaked when he pushed it open, its rusty hinges protesting.

Outside the summer breeze was warm. It kissed their cheeks in the purple, star-shimmered twilight, bringing with it the scent of damp earth, grass, and decay. The church graveyard was a tumbled maze of tombstones and crypts.

"Now we shall see through a glass, darkly. Come," the priest said.

His words paralyzed her. Could she be as strong as he

and face herself in the glass, not running away as she always had before?

He tapped the whip to his boot, and she went with him to where a lone light beckoned in the distance—a lantern affixed to a tall wooden cross, the marker for a grave in the center of the cemetery, set upon a gentle rise.

"Step up. Face the cross."

She obeyed, and he lay upon her, fitting himself into the parted crease of her ass as she clung to the cross, prickles of pain blooming on her bare chest and arms as tiny splinters pierced her skin. His leather-covered fingers trailed over her body, sweeping her hair from her back. He gave her bottom an almost casual caress and the tiniest of slaps, resting his hand on the curve of it as he kissed her neck and licked a tiny spot above her nape. She felt the warm slither of his tongue and goose bumps rose to meet it.

She worried she might pass out, blissed and lulled by his touch, but was alert again immediately when he whispered in her ear, "Lower your skirt to your knees. Press your cunt against the cross."

She unzipped her skirt with trembling hands, pushing it down to her knees, spreading them wider to keep it in place.

She was amazed at the ever constant shifting of her feelings. The desire to flee, the desire to come, the desire to do anything the priest asked rapidly changed places.

"Press close. Do it for me," he said.

Again, with only the slightest hesitation, she responded, pressing harder into the splintered cross. Pain stung her breasts and her fingers when she reached to curl them around the crossbar.

She shuddered, a feeling of complete surrender washing through her. She imagined her sins swept away in the flood and was comforted, calmed.

"Hold on tight," the priest said, unclipping the leash and

tossing it away. He clasped a shorter chain to the front of the collar and then to the cross, holding Katie on a tighter tether, leaving her enough slack to turn if she were required to but not enough to keep her from strangling should she fall.

He crouched, sliding his palms over her hips, fondling the tender creases behind her knees and the smooth flesh of her inner thighs. He eased her skirt, sandals, and panties off, leaving her naked, facing the cross.

"Who dares shed man's blood, by man shall have his blood shed."

The priest lifted his hands to the crossbar, his fingers brushing Katie's thumb in a comforting sweep. He reached between her legs and dragged his fingertips over her cunt. Her flesh felt puffy, throbbing, her clit lush and swollen. He gave it a flicker.

The priest used her hair to turn her head. She shivered, looking into his obsidian eyes, drowning in his words.

"Your penance," he said, "will be your sins . . . repaid with your pain given to me. Sin. Atonement. Rapture." His gaze held Katie's as firmly as his leather-covered fingers held her cunt.

Katie felt a new surge of adrenaline clash deliciously with her aching need.

"*Dominus vobiscum. Et cum spirito tuo.* Bless you," he said.

She held tighter to the cross, closing her eyelids tight, her pussy convulsing in the priest's hand as he gave it one last squeeze.

"Do you know a prayer?"

"The Lord's Prayer is the only one I know by heart." Her voice trembled.

"Say it."

She began, her voice quivering, "Our Father, who art in heaven, hallowed be thy name."

"This will hurt. Hold on and pray," he said, before stepping away.

"Thy kingdom come. Thy will be done, on earth as it is in heaven." Katie's body stiffened, and she pressed harder into the cross, wanting and fearing, guilt-ridden yet needing this so badly she ached, her longing awakened fully and begging for release.

She heard a whoosh of sound—whip through air. She felt a single mark cut into her flesh high on the left side of her back, just above the jut of her shoulder bone. She imagined the straight slash of welted skin crying blood tears, black shimmers, and she screamed.

"Go on." His voice was calm.

"Give us this day our daily bread and forgive us our trespasses, as we forgive those who trespass against us!"

He waited for her to quiet before delivering another strike of the whip, leaving a new slash of pain on the upper right side of her back. Again, he waited for her screams to stop before adding to his creation, forming—with quick whip strokes—what she pictured as twin crosses carved into the flesh of her back.

"And lead us not into temptation, but deliver us from evil," she said, her knees shaking as she hugged the cross to keep from falling and being choked by the collar and short chain.

The priest came to her, his hands sweeping tender and leather cool over her shivering body. He turned her to face him and kissed her mouth tenderly. She tasted her tears when their tongues met.

"Truth and mercy have come together. Righteousness and peace have kissed."

He crouched, leaving her breathless, his dark gaze resting on the wet, pink splay of her cunt.

He kissed it, rubbing her slick offering over his parted lips.

"Atonement," he said, his breath a warm flutter on Katie's clit. A flicker of his tongue followed the curve of its hood, easing it up and down.

Her cheeks flooded with color, her pain already fading. A thrilling surge of emotion threatened to spill over into a rapturous orgasm, or a wild struggle to be free.

She knew she had the power to reach up and unclasp the leash, to run away or simply ask to be let go, but she didn't do any of these things. She wanted it all. She needed it. Groaning, overcome by the intense gratification the priest's touch gave her, she pushed forward against his mouth.

"Rapture," Katie sighed as the priest lapped the nectar droplets from her slit, his tongue a wet, slithering heat.

"Give the rest to me. Let it go. Finish," he said, pulling off his leather gloves.

He spread her legs wider as he pressed the cluster of his fingers into her, not stopping until they were deeply buried, hooked and pressing into a place that made her insides quiver.

His tongue snaked in a languid twirl through the furls of her pussy and over the knob of her clit, sliding up and down in firm knowing strokes timed with the thrusts of his fingers into her cunt. His mouth was hot, his tongue gliding with velvety strokes. His teeth raked, and he suckled until her legs began to buckle and her body accepted all of his hand.

"For yours is the kingdom, the power, and the glory of the Father, the Son, and the Holy Spirit, now and forever. Amen." Katie finished the prayer, her voice ragged, panted moans as she came—a surge into the priest's mouth. Pushing closer, shuddering release, her cunt gripped his fist as spasms of pleasure washed over her in waves. Cresting, they left in their wake a new sense of peace.

When he pulled his hand from her, she felt a trickle of come slide down her thigh like a tear she no longer needed.

"*Dominus noster Saint Michael te absolvat et ego auctoritate ipsius te absolvo,*" the priest said in a low and final tone after the last pulse died.

He stood, his gaze warm as he kissed Katie's cheeks and freed her. Enfolding her in his arms, he held her close, soothing her.

"As a man thinks in his heart, so is he. Be free, Katie O'Malley."

He unclasped her leash, but the collar remained—an anchor as the priest led Katie away, absolved.

AMETHYST'S FEATHER

Once upon a time, in a land not so very far away, there was a fairytale princess of a girl named Amethyst. She was fair of face and form and so, had many admirers.

Odes were written about her beauty—hundreds just about her eyes, which were described as aqua, ocean, and lapis. Whatever their color—often dependent upon her mood—everyone agreed that to look into them was to fall in love.

Some of her love-struck swains would wait until she rose from a chair, only to sit upon it and bask in her fading warmth. They would look for single, precious strands of her hair and keep them like treasures.

Grown men lay in beds next to willing wives and refused to touch them. They preferred to close their eyes and dream of the way Amethyst would respond if only a man might be lucky enough to touch her vanilla-scented skin. The deviant among them spun feverish fantasies where she knelt at their feet, doing things unholy at their whim.

Many wore bruised knees from fervent prayers for even a smile from her rosebud lips. Some struck bargains with the devil (who profited greatly from her refusal to bestow even the slightest hope upon anyone).

Amethyst did not know any of these things and, had she known, she'd not have cared; though she moved, sat, spoke, and sometimes even looked her suitors in the eyes, her mind was elsewhere, along with her heart.

The jealous said she was stuck-up. The spiteful said she was too stupid to know of the stir she caused all around her. The envious said people were only attracted to her because she was so detached from all of them; her beauty overshadowed by her coldness.

None of these things was true.

Amethyst was lost in daydreams of a time when she had been a chubby cheeked child, just beginning to bloom into a woman. She had climbed over a towering wall and run away, her spirit of adventure taking over her good sense, her mother said later.

She had gotten lost in the primordial forest surrounding her home, wandering for a day and a night in the cold unknown.

She stopped when she could go no further, one of her dainty, bejeweled shoes gone astray. Her feet were cut and blistered, her dress torn and dirty. The long, red hair boys would someday write poems about a cloak of ratted tangles she wrapped around herself for warmth.

When the moon rose high in the sky on the second night, she huddled in the hollow of a welcoming tree, making a pillow from fallen leaves. She cried pitiful tears until she fell into a fitful, exhausted slumber.

When she woke it was darker than dark, and colder than cold, but it was far from quiet. She heard many noises—the skitter of tiny toenails on bark, wind whispering through trees, owls hooting. But the noise that alarmed her—made her sit up straight, ears tuned—was the sound of heavy footsteps coming closer and closer until finally they stopped, right by her shallow hiding place.

Amethyst whimpered and squeezed her eyes closed, sinking as far as she could into the sheltering tree. She prayed in this moment of terror, not to any god but to her mother.

When she dared peek to see what had come for her, she saw a man. Crouched, peering into the tree, he was illuminated by moonlight. His face was handsome, his expression calm, but he was a stranger.

She looked at him, a fat tear rolling down her cheek. The man reached into the darkness and captured it on the tip of his finger. It shimmered there like a jewel, bewitching Amethyst and drawing her cautiously from her hiding place.

She allowed herself to be soothed and gathered into his arms. He lifted her atop his fine horse, a wildly beautiful creature. There was no saddle yet, when they settled upon its back, she found the seat most comfortable; she lay perfectly nestled within the man's arms, her bottom snug against his thighs.

He was slender, his age hard to tell. He looked young in some ways, wise and old in others. He was tall. His hair was very long, very dark. His eyes were hauntingly beautiful. His touch was gentle.

Amethyst decided to trust him and relaxed her body against his as they made their way through the forest, and over the fields of heather surrounding her home.

It was only later she realized she had not told him where she lived or spoken a single word to him, not even a 'thank you'.

As they rode, he talked to her, his breath warm on her flushed cheeks. He told her stories of far-off places and magical things. He wove tales of a life that might be had one day for a fairytale princess of a girl, and a man with no home. He spoke of love, passion and happily-ever-after. He hinted at grownup things they might do together or, even with others. He said no matter what, he would always belong to her, and she to him.

She listened, turning her face into his chest. No one had ever spoken to her of such things. Her mother had only talked of the love between a husband and his proper wife, and of the necessary coupling that would result in children.

Amethyst listened to the man speak of other things and imagined every one in vivid detail. She'd thought she was all alone in her secret desires, a very bad girl for dreaming of and longing for such wickedness, but he made her feel safe, understood. He made her feel as though anything were possible.

By the time the strange man rode away, leaving Amethyst at her garden gate, she was in love. Spellbound and overwhelmed by emotion, she was never able to think of much else as she grew up.

She never cared about the boys and girls who looked at her with such want, was never moved by the songs sung to her beauty, and never dreamed of another. She just waited, dreaming of his return; she knew he would come for her someday. He had promised. He had whispered his name into her ear before he left, like a secret, and tucked a raven feather into her hand.

She never told anyone what happened while she'd been lost; they had no idea the incident had forever changed her. No one pushed her to speak of it, and soon everyone forgot the adventure that haunted her.

When she was a grown woman, her father decided it was long past time for her to marry. As was the custom, he picked her husband, not worrying at all over what she might feel about his selection. He chose a man who had a fine reputation and lands benefiting him in their joining with his own.

When Amethyst was told her father's plan, she wept for days. She cried so many tears the creek twining through her garden became a river of salted water that did not evaporate until she was long dead. Every bloom in her garden withered to dust, except for the lilacs; these flowers bloomed lusher than ever before.

She dared not tell her father of her daydreams or of the girlish crush she still carried within her heart, but she held the raven feather like a talisman, and prayed day and night.

On her wedding day, she was a vision in virgin white. Her skin was winter-pale, all color gone from her cheeks; the blood in her had rushed to her heart, which seemed to cry out with every beat for her man with no home.

As her father led her down the aisle to her husband, each step she took was heavy. Halfway there, she looked up into the eyes of the man chosen for her. He smiled, a handsome smile. He looked happy.

She knew he had a good soul. He had spoken to Amethyst during his "courtship" of his hopes and dreams, of the children they would raise, the contented life they would lead. He was a nice man, a kind man, a man very like her father. Everyone agreed they were perfectly matched.

Amethyst slowed. Her father frowned, tightening his grip on her arm. She looked back, over her shoulder, just as a raven flew into the church, pushed by a howling wind that opened the heavy doors with a bang. The bird shrieked, a haunting cry that pierced the serene harp music, its breast tinted violet by a stained-glass window that cast a shard of splintered light upon its heart.

Amethyst stopped, looking up at her startled father. She kissed his cheek and whispered, "Forgive me," before picking up her skirts and running as fast as she could out of the church.

No one chased her, not at first, so shocked were they. So she was quite alone when she finally slowed, as lost as she had been when she was a child, deep within the great woods.

Her cheeks were stained with tears, and she was blind to the path she left behind her; bits of wedding dress littered the forest floor, lace and finery, something old, something new, something borrowed and something blue, burnished strands of hair dotted with seed pearls. Her veil fluttered like a flag in the treetops until the wind blew it far, far away.

She wondered if she could find the hollowed out tree, the very one in which she had hidden as a child. If she succeeded, would he come for her then? Would he find her there?

She searched all through the day and into the night, stopping only when she could not take another step. She fell to her knees, in a meadow dotted with lavender, and made the grass there her bed, the purple wildflowers her pillow. She drifted into a deep, deep sleep.

When she woke, it was darker than dark and colder than cold, but it was far from quiet. She heard the sounds of the night—the whir of Night Herons, the stirring of leaves moved by the breeze, and finally, faint footfalls.

When she opened her eyes, she knew she was being watched; the tiny hairs on the back of her neck stood at tingled attention. She held her breath, cautious, flattening herself upon the ground. Her weak night-vision saw nothing until a wolf stepped into the clearing and was illuminated by moonlight.

He was raven black and, even from where she sat, she could see his eyes were hauntingly beautiful; they reflected the moonlight, glowing silver. They seemed to lure her, those eyes, to draw her in, and so she rose, walking to him as if in a trance.

He waited until she'd almost reached him, then he turned away. Amethyst followed, without thought or fear, through the maze of trees to an even deeper, darker part of the forest.

Try as she might, she could never quite catch up with the wolf, though her fingers ached to touch his fur, and she wanted just one more glimpse of his eyes. She had to hurry to stay with him, pushing the branches away that reached for her like fingers, like lovers.

He led her to a perfectly rounded clearing in the thick forest. Surrounded by large, purposefully placed stones, the place reminded her of something; the memory tugged at her. The wolf rounded a tree set in the middle of the circle, an ancient, craggy, twisted thing. She followed him through a maze of gnarled, half-dead branches. In some places, she had to crawl, for the limbs dipped so low they almost touched the ground.

"Stop," she called to the black wolf, wanting to rest, to cling to him, to make him explain what was going on. She followed him one last time around the enormous trunk of the old tree, and when she came to the other side, he was gone as if he had never been there at all.

Amethyst began to cry, slumping against the rough bark. Her anguished tears wet the mossy, verdant ground at her feet. Rooted tendrils sprang from the earth, winding around her ankles. Whip-thin sucker branches slid around her, circling her waist and wrists. Before she could so much as move a muscle, she was bound tight to the tree trunk, her hands lifted high, and her feet spread wide. She was unable to do more than wiggle and scream, her loud cries scaring the birds from the trees; their black silhouettes drowned out the moon's light.

This time, in her moment of utter terror, she did not pray to God or her mother; she prayed to her love, and this time he came.

He walked to her, laying a finger on her tear-streaked cheek. He slid his hand into the bodice of her gown, his fingers curling over her heart's racing beat as if to soothe it. He cupped her breast, brushing his thumb over her nipple.

She stilled, so many questions falling away, swallowed in the storm his touch on her body stirred. She only wanted more, more of whatever he would give her. She was afraid if she gave into the need raging inside for answers, he would leave, so when he drew a knife and cut her tattered wedding dress away, she did nothing more than shudder against the cold blade.

He smiled at her for the first time, and it was like watching the sun come up after a long, dark night; his face lit with it, became boyish. She wondered how old he was. He'd not changed at all from her memory of him. That was odd, wasn't it? She felt drugged, the time before, and the time now somehow melting together until all she knew was this moment, bound to this tree, naked, just a fairytale princess of a girl offering herself to this strange man she loved with all of her soul.

"Please," she finally said, the word coming from her before she could stop it, a plea for something she did not understand and could not name.

He didn't ask what she begged for. She understood this was not because he did not care, but because he knew. He laid his body full upon her, covering her with his warmth. He smoothed her hair, freeing each tangle as his mouth found hers and suckled a path to the pulse on her throat. He reached between her legs to cup the downy soft red fur there, tugging until the mound beneath his palm plumped, swelling. His fingers dipped inside, finding the petals of her sex slick and wet.

She moaned, arching into him, wanting this, wanting him, saying again, "Please."

He spoke to her softly in the husky voice she remembered so well; he told her how he had waited for her to seek him out, how he had needed to be invited, needed to be asked here. He said her wishes were made sacred by her tears. He told her of his loneliness.

His touch became more insistent. Something hard pressed to her stomach, and two of his fingers slid up inside her. She felt a clench of dull pain, a flow of virgin blood and pangs of fear, darkly exciting.

She writhed against him. He stilled her, his sharp teeth piercing the skin of her breast, making the tiniest of marks near her heart. He lapped at the droplet of blood that welled, laving her nipples with his tongue and nibbling on them when they rose, as if in offering to him.

She liked it, this back and forth between want and fear, pleasure and pain, but as he worked his fingers into her—even as the desire in her blossomed into a living thing that gripped her belly and made her insides shake—her mind screamed as if trying to wake her from a nightmare.

"No," she said, the word bubbling up with a will of its own. She heard her mother's voice and the echoes of all the girls she had grown up with. Surely none of them would feel as she did, surely they would not want the things she craved. They would be afraid. They would be modest. They would be good.

"No," he repeated as if the word was foreign. He parted her lips with his, sharing his breath with her, drinking from her mouth until Amethyst was light-headed, grateful for the bindings that held her fast.

He grasped the hard thing pressing into her belly, sliding it between her thighs. With his other hand, he lifted her bottom, tilting her hips. His turgid, hot flesh nudged her sex. "But, you invited me, beloved. You belong to me; there is no going back," he said, kissing her again, his mouth lush on hers.

She reveled in his touch and drowned in the moonlit

gleam of his eyes. She felt the brush of his long, dark hair caressing her breasts like silken butterflies as he leaned into her and she knew he was right, no matter what anyone else might think.

She moaned as he pressed against her. She opened herself to him and the roots that bound her fell away. Clinging to him, winding her hands in his hair and her legs around his waist, the whole world faded away, and everything came down to just the two of them, flesh to flesh.

A loud gunshot rang out in the forest, reality slamming through Amethyst's sensual haze. She slumped against her strange lover and fell to the forest floor, in a dead faint.

The last thing she heard was the sound of his anguished cry as he crashed through the brush, running away. The last thing she felt was the wetness of her lust, slipping down her inner-thigh, like a kiss.

When she woke, she looked up into a kind face. She recognized him, the man who was to have been her husband. She found she could not meet his gaze. She cried, closing her eyes, letting him lift her into his arms, letting him take her home.

Everything now seemed so clear. She felt like a true fairytale princess awakened after one hundred years of sleep to find everything changed.

Her betrothed told her he loved her and would wait for her to be well; he said everything was going to be all right. He handed her over to her mother, who enfolded her in caring arms, bathed her, and left her tucked safely in her bed, alone with her memories and thoughts.

It was only later Amethyst realized she had not said a single word to her rescuer, not even a 'thank you'.

She thought of her husband-to-be, of the promise in his eyes, the sincerity of his love offering. She wondered if she had a future with him, and envisioned a life much like the one she had always known, like the one her parents shared, like the one all the girls she knew wanted so badly.

She thought of the years she had spent dreaming of that day so long ago, when she'd been lost in the forest. She thought of the wolf, of the tree, of the things she'd felt there. She remembered the pain and the secret pleasure, the shame, the desire, and the love.

She imagined what everyone else would think, but most of all, she contemplated what she thought and before night became dawn, Amethyst knew what she had to do.

She gathered her most precious things—the raven feather, a tiny glass sailboat, and a necklace with a silver heart strung from it.

She left behind a note for her parents, telling them she loved them, that she would be back someday if they could accept her into their hearts, no matter what paths she walked.

This time she did not climb the great wall and sneak away; she walked right through the garden, past the fragrant lilacs, and over the river of tears, out the gate.

Amethyst wandered into the night, knowing she might never find the hollowed out tree, the meadow where she had slept, or the ancient oak surrounded by magical stones.

There was much she did not understand, but she knew her lover would find her, wherever she was. She belonged to him as surely as the stars belonged to the night.

SMOKE AND MIRRORS

S he burned Gauloises cigarettes like incense because, she said, the scent reminded her of home.

Though Monique had come from Paris with her mother when she was only five, and was half Russian, she was as unmistakably French as the Eiffel Tower. Maybe it was the way her mermaid's eyes tilted at the corners, or the proud set of her head atop her ballerina's neck, or the whimsical tilt of her luxuriant mouth. Whatever it was, I was entranced from the moment we met.

Her tiny closet of an apartment on the Lower East Side was a testament to her loyalty to all things French and enough to tell me ridicule would have ended our friendship.

Her cushions were swathed in thrift-store toile. Screens painted with scenes of Montmartre and the Seine covered the reality of New York outside her haven. Red wine, cheese, and bread were her preferred sustenance. She nursed pots of lavender de Provence and fragrant thyme on the fire escape in the summer and saw them through the winter with the love of a mother.

Monique listened to Piaf on an old turntable because, she explained, without the crackles and snaps of a record album being caressed by a needle, the music was not "right". That long hot summer, making love in her iron, curlicued bed, I began to agree with her.

"*Ah, mon chéri, tu es tant sexy!*" she purred.

I didn't understand most of what she said in French, but it didn't matter. Anything that came out of her mouth was titillating to me.

Piaf sang *Sous le ciel de Paris*, and I reclined like an emperor while Monique devoured me.

Usually, our lovemaking was a back and forth tussle for control. At various times, she would give in, or I would, or we'd just melt together in a tangle of body parts. We fucked like people with no modesty, no shame, and no boundaries. Sometimes it was hard and fast, over in a flash. Other times we lasted all day, occasionally spending entire weekends naked, fucking, eating, talking, and listening to music.

Our relationship was still new, but I had a feeling it would always be this way. We just seemed to fit one another in every way, both physical and mental. I know everyone in the throes of new love says things like that, but with us, it was true. I knew no matter what happened my life would never be the same.

"*Comme tu es joli, chéri. Voyez, comme il dort maintenant. Est-il fatigué, le pauvre petit? Mais voistu! Il se revéille! Il lève la tête! Ah, comme il est beau, ton petit soldat. Mais non, il n'est pas petit, pas soldat, il est tout un général, ta queue!*" she said, in between licks and sucks of my cock. Her tongue was a snake in the Garden of Eden, tempting and seductive, winding its way down my shaft.

"What?" I said, my voice taut with sexual tension. I closed my eyes and still was assaulted with daydream images of her. She was like a drug I could not get enough of, could not stop thinking of and wanting.

She kept me on the edge, fingers and tongue working together. The sound was obscene—wet slithers, sucking strokes and heavily accented English that drove me wild.

"It was silly, *mon loup*," she said, her lips forming a moue as she kissed the aubergine, mushroom-head of my cock. Her lush bottom lip shone with a gloss of my pre-cum.

"Nothing you say is silly, Minette. Tell me." I loved that nickname—sex kitten. It fit her perfectly and made her purr every time I said it.

She sighed softly, her head coming to rest on my thigh, her fingers cradling my turgid prick, those cat-like green eyes turned up to meet mine. "I was talking about your cock. How pretty it is. I said, look how he sleeps. I asked if he was tired, the poor little thing. But, then he woke and lifted his head and I said he was beautiful, your little soldier. But, he isn't little, and not merely a soldier. No. He is a general, your cock!" She blushed as she finished, laughing softly and kissing my balls.

Tiny hairs rose to meet her lips, and my flesh quivered. I was so close to coming that just her breath wafting over my penis was almost enough to set me off. I had to grip the sheets, and think of the Yankees, to keep from spurting all over her pretty face.

Like any good general, I accepted my minion's worship and took control. My fingers fisted in her hair, luxurious locks of red twisted around and around until she was poised where I wanted her, over my cock once more. I urged her mouth downward, slowly, to tease us both. "Open wide, Minette. Make me come." My voice was gruff, commanding. I was in charge, and we both knew it.

I let her hair fall to my thighs, framing her face with its waves. She moaned, swiveling her head and corkscrewing up and down my cock. "Faster. Deeper," I instructed her, lifting my hips to show her the way I wanted it until she fell into the metronomic rhythm I imposed upon her.

"*Oui, oui, mon coeur*," she said when she came up for breath, her voice husky from the ramming of my cock down her throat and her own building desire.

She wrapped her arms around my torso, nails scratching lightly over my belly. I twisted and began to buck until her mouth almost took in my entire cock. I felt her nose buried in my pubic hair and her teeth graze my fuck-lusted skin.

"Fuck!" I shouted, taking her head between my hands, and fucking her face like a street whore's.

I was rough. So was she. I felt her long legs spread on the bed, silken skin against mine, as she almost crawled in place, wanting, it seemed, to crawl right inside of me.

Crazed with lust, my body bowed, I spread my knees wide and gushed into her eager little mouth. I kept going and going until her mouth was full, leaking at the corners. I groaned as she licked the droplets from her lips and smiled at me, coming up to lie atop my body, her curves fitting me perfectly.

"*Je t'adore. Je t'aime*," she said, for the first time, her head atop my heart, which still beat frantically even as my orgasm died.

I knew enough French to understand that, and my battered heart sang. "I love you too, Monique."

The images, smells, and memories are still so alive in me; sometimes it's as if I could reach through the ether of time and step back, to that walk-up flat filled with France and the only woman I've ever loved.

I was not her first lover, but unlike most couples giddy with new love, we didn't share our former experiences, successes and failures. It was as if, when our eyes met, we knew everything truly important there was to know about each other, and the details of how we'd arrived there didn't matter.

Instead, we spent our time learning about one another through touch, taste, scent, and sex. When my fingers slipped over the bumps of her fragile spine and my palms filled with the ripe peach of her ass, it was as if puzzle pieces clicked into place, and I was given all the knowledge of her I needed. Looking into her eyes, I saw myself mirrored and was home with another for the first time. Nothing else mattered.

I'd climb her stairs, enter her recreated Paris, and the rest of the world would fade away.

We ate dinner in bed more often than not, and after feeding one another tidbits, licking the crumbs from our fingers, and drinking wine offered from the cups of our mouths. After, she'd light her Gauloises cigarettes, and the room would fill with wisps of gossamer smoke. The dark tobacco gave off a distinctive aroma, the scent rich and earthy. Soon I began to associate its unique bouquet with Monique, fucking, and France.

Monique offered herself to me as the final course of our meals. Spreading her long, dancer's legs, she drew me down to her and into a world of sensual pleasures. Chevalier and Piaf sang accompaniment to the sex-symphony we created in her bed.

She had a childlike figure, surprisingly frail in one so crackling with energy. Her skin was translucent, white. I loved to make the blush rise in her face, and see her neck and chest pinken because of the scratch of my day's growth of beard, and the completeness of my attention to her pleasure.

There was no part of her I did not lick, or pinch, spank or fondle. I inserted myself into her every orifice, and she into mine. We had a mutual need to be as close as possible and nothing was forbidden between us.

Slick with sweat, in the hottest days of summer, our bodies slid together in a way that seemed almost primal, primitive as if in the act of fucking we became something else. Reduced to our baser natures as humans, we elevated our individual selves to something beyond what I thought most people would ever know. We fused.

Monique did not smoke, but liked to hold cigarettes for me while I inhaled and blew the vapors over her body in warm streams and billows that caressed the furrow between her thighs, making her shiver. I learned that the nicotine prolonged my erection somehow and the head-rush I got from the tobacco added to my sense of drifting somewhere far away and exotically foreign.

It was seductive, the smoke. Had I known where one could indulge in opium, lounging on plush sofas, nursing hookah pipes, I'd have saved every penny to go there with Monique. I wanted to float with her in a smoke-filled dream where anything was possible, and nothing else mattered. Instead, I smoked Gauloises as we drank cheap, table wine, and was as close to heaven as I've ever come here on earth.

Her walls were a deep crimson, and she did not like artificial lights, choosing instead to burn cheap wax candles that only added to my sense of being somewhere much more compelling than the world I'd known before. Smoke wafted in tendrils of gray and white over red and toile backgrounds and the smell of burning wax mingled with other scents— sex, cigarettes, Monique's seductive perfume.

Her cunt smelled of the ocean-fresh, salty tang mingled with musky water scents. After a day of fucking, she would smell like me. I liked her that way. It was as if I branded her, not only with the marks I left on her pale skin, but also with my very essence.

As the summer wound to a close, life began to press upon

me, intruding into the little world we'd formed together. A new semester of school needed my planning, and my parents demanded a visit. Friends whom I had not seen in months started leaving notes on my doorstep, worried when I failed to return any of their calls and never showed up at our regular haunts. People summered on Long Island without me.

Lying on her floor, nose to nose, my hands wandered over the wondrous bounty of her skin and, inside my head, an imaginary camera recorded every detail. There . . . a mole shaped like a lopsided heart. Here, the silk of her hair slipping through my fingers. Everywhere, lovely woman. Sexy and sure of her charms. A coquette with a mermaid's face and a siren's allure.

"*Fais-moi disparaître*," she whispered, her mouth moving over my lips, her fingers twisting in my hair.

"What?" I asked, though I did not really care, not then, what she said.

"*Fais-moi jouir.*" She tangled her fingers in mine and dragged them down, over her belly, urging them between her legs, which she spread wide.

I understood.

I love to fuck. I love to kiss and taste my lover, but there is something so tactile about using my fingers to pleasure her. Though my cock is sensitive, it cannot compare to the way every nerve on the tips of my fingers feels her every furl, her every slick petal. The moment when she swells with want, when her body oozes its juice onto my hand is one I cherish, knowing I am pleasuring her. I hold her close, my mouth near enough to dip down, my teeth catching an up-tilted nipple and biting until she writhes against me, pressing her pubis into my flicking fingers.

My cock was so hard, leaking against her hip, but I concentrated on her, that camera inside my head recording every moment as if it might be the last. I wanted to bury myself deep within her, impaling her and forcing her to stay with me always, but I waited. It was as if I knew these moments might need to be stretched out to last a lifetime, and I wanted to savor each one.

"*Oui! Oui! Maintenant! Je jouis!*" she cried. I'm coming!

"Come with me, Minette. Come," I whispered into the curve of her shoulder, fingers bearing down harder now, knowing she could take whatever I gave in these final moments before she exploded.

When I slapped her quivering, wet pussy, she lifted from the floor and shouted, "*Baise-moi! Baise-moi!*" Fuck me! Fuck me!

I did. I fucked her, flipping her over onto her knees and pushing her face into the floor, my pussy-wet hand on the back of her neck. I plowed into her like a man who has never fucked before and may never have the chance again. I left marks on her hips that day, bruises from the force of my fingers digging into her flesh, pulling her to me and pushing her away, only to pull her back and bury myself within her once more. I felt like screaming. Like crying. Like dying.

She accepted what I gave her, even when my cock left her warm cunt and buried itself in her tight bottom.

She screamed and moaned until my hand moved around to find her cunt again, fingers moving exactly the way I knew she needed them to.

"*Oui, oui, comme ça!*"

I made the pain go away, and we came together. After, we collapsed, entwined upon the floor.

"I love you," I said, smoothing tendrils of hair from her sweat-soaked temples.

The red walls of her apartment sheltering us, satiated and exhausted, we slept as Piaf sang lullabies.

Now, many years later, my walls are the same shade of red. My windows are covered with painted screens, and I burn candles and Gauloises. Inside, I burn for what was and for what I lost when the inevitable came, and Monique left me for her first love—Paris.

Every evening, I climb my stairs and close the door on the rest of my world. Late at night, I stand in front of a floor-to-ceiling mirror, smoking, and spinning old, French records while I pleasure myself, needing the acrid smoke in my lungs, and the scent of it in my nostrils to accompany my hand's jerking of my cock.

Behind me, I see Notre Dame, Pigalle, and the Seine cutting through charming streets. If I squint in the candle-light and smoke-filled room, just as I come, I see her. I can believe the painted image of Monique hanging on the wall behind me, and reflected in the mirror, is her. She urges me to one more orgasm and, in those moments, I find her again in the haze. I am the young man she once loved.

I sing along to the music, translating as I go—give your heart and soul to me and life will always be *la vie en rose*—and sometimes I cry.

PAGANINI'S MUSE

Sebastian's manager pounded on his dressing room door; the beating of his fisted hands became percussion to the song Sebastian played on and on—bluesy and throbbing, sexual and haunting. The melody alternately cajoled and demanded, seduced and enchanted.

Gifted, he was the current darling of the concert world. Radical and unorthodox, he was just as likely to play Black Sabbath as Paganini; he was a rock star in a world of staid classical musicians.

As he played, his fingers ached. The blood within them pulsed, as if wanting to burst free of his skin and flow, crimson, down his hand. His arm was numb though it flew, carrying the bow over the strings, frantically ricocheting back and forth, wringing the notes from his instrument. He caressed the fingerboard, touching it the way some men would a woman's flesh. The Guarnerius violin was his muse's favorite. When he played it, he felt her near.

He ignored the knocking on his door and disregarded the cries of his name—Sebastian . . . Lachance . . . Sebastian . . . Lachance. Girls shouted from the alley below—fans waiting by the stage door, their nubile young bodies pressed to his sleek black Rolls Royce as if the chrome and metal held a piece of him.

It was always the same, in every city, after every performance.

Tonight, he'd played his music and left his admirers screaming for more. He'd kissed a few groupies as he left the stage. He'd accepted the flowers, the panties, and the hotel keys. He'd even signed a few autographs and posed for pictures with a charming old woman from Milan and her moon-faced daughter. What more did they want?

Come. Come. Come, he thought now, closing his eyes, pushing visions of his manager, the concert, and his fans out of his mind; his muse would never come if he concentrated on anything other than her.

He played louder, drowning out the frantic knocking and the chanting outside by pressing his bow harder into the strings, dragging it closer to the bridge so the violin screamed. The sound filled his head and vibrated against his shoulder. Soon, he forgot everything but his need and his music.

He was desperate, hungry, and half-crazed. He'd do anything to lure her.

Couldn't she feel it? Couldn't she hear him begging? Hadn't he done enough?

"Please . . . please . . . please!" he shouted as he played. "Anything, for you!"

He played until finally she appeared—when he was dripping with sweat, on his knees, barely able to hold the quivering violin anymore.

She cradled his head to her belly, her red fingernails sliding through his hair, skimming the wet slick of his scalp.

The voices outside faded away. She brought calm with her, peace.

Her lips pressed to his forehead. "I am here, my love."

The timbre of her voice was harmonious with the song

in his heart. Her presence cast a net about him, pulled tight, constricting and fluttering around his heart. His cock stiffened in his pants as his fingers clutched at her.

"Thank you." He pressed kisses to her mons, to the puffy swell of it under her gossamer dress. He dared a lick, following the curl of a pubic hair he could feel in hyper-relief through the fabric of her gown.

Sebastian shuddered, his entire body thrumming like a penis aching to explode. Everything in him felt new again, alive despite his exhaustion, and tuned into her, his beautiful muse.

"Muse, Muse, Muse," he sighed, closing his eyes.

She allowed him to bunch up her skirt with his fingers. He delved beneath, sliding his hands over her smooth, white thighs, over the succulent mounds of her clefted ass. He licked the hollow nestled against her pussy, the crack between it and her leg and inhaled the scent of her—woman, musk, flowers.

"Yes, my darling," she said, drawing his head back with fingers that grew tighter in his long, brown hair.

His tongue resonated with her taste; he licked his lips and swooned, drugged with it. He looked up into her face, almost loathing to drag his gaze from her sex.

Each time he saw her was like the first. She wove a spell around him, haunting him. She was mystical, magical, and otherworldly. Her aura glowed brightly, like the wings of a hummingbird—moving so fast only he could see its rainbow colors. He had to look at her through the slit of his lashes. She brushed them with her fingertips.

"You played so well tonight," she said, slipping one of her fingers into his mouth.

He suckled gratefully, listening to her. His knees ached from kneeling, but the rest of him was free of pain or concern. She was here. Nothing else mattered. And tonight, he was going to fuck her.

"Pizzicato, harmonics, technical wizardry. Godlike." She strung the words together like a poem.

He wanted to kiss her feet and would have had she not bent to him, her lush mouth brushing his, her hands cupping his face. Her hair drifted around them both, a red cloud that blocked out everything, sheltering them.

"For you, Muse. All for you," Sebastian answered, drowning in her aqua gaze.

Her eyes narrowed and she pushed him away.

His violin clattered to the floor, his bow still clutched in his hand.

"You lie. You play for them too," she said, flinging an angry gesture to the open window, where the girls still crooned to him, begging him to come down, come out, come away with them.

"Nooo . . ." he protested, shaking the long dark locks that made him a favorite of poster-makers and scandal magazines. He crawled to her. "It's you I play for!"

"Do you love me?" She closed the window, locking it. She curled her fingers, beckoning him close once more.

Sebastian rose to his feet, taking her in his arms. He pulled her to him, seeing in her eyes that she liked it this way—when he acted as if she was just a woman. Just a girl.

She was so much smaller than him, her body so much softer. He dipped his head, his breath ruffling her hair, his tongue casting temptation upon her collarbone.

She moaned when his hand found the plump perfection of her breast.

"I love only you, Muse," he whispered into the part of her lips. He held her nape in the clench of his fingers, stealing a kiss and her breath along with it.

He danced with her, twirling her slowly around the room. He made it a tango and a waltz, and a dirty dance, grinding himself into her then pulling away. He kissed her, winding her hair around his arm. He cast his own spell upon her with his gypsy-eyes and fluid limbs, and soon she melted into his embrace, into the dance, into him. Just a woman.

There was a couch, there were chairs, there was the floor, but he pushed her against the door, where his manager still knocked, frantically calling to him. Sebastian felt the wood resonate with the sound as he laid her back against it. Rending her dress with one rip from neck to hem, he bared her spun-sugar skin to his gaze, to his hand, to his lust.

He kissed her as if his life depended on it, sealing his mouth to hers, stroking her tongue with his own, velvety hot. He thrust his hands into her witch-red hair, holding her still for his plundering exploration of her mouth.

"They say I've lost my mind, that I've gone mad," he said, his tongue following the path of her breast. It made him ache in the pit of his stomach—the sweetness of the slope of skin from her breast to her nipple. He'd never seen anything so beautiful. He laved the warm pink flesh of her areola with his tongue. Reaching down, he unzipped his pants, wrapping his fist around his turgid penis, pumping it with his hand. He let her feel it against her belly, let her feel how huge she'd made him. He wanted her to ache for it.

Her head bounced on the wood as the efforts of his manager were joined by Sebastian's pleading assistant.

Shaking his head as if to clear it, he kissed his muse impatiently. Fuck everything else, fuck them all. He needed this, needed her, now.

He hooked his fingers under her knee, dragging it up to ride his hip. She shuddered as he spread her wide, the knob of his prick splitting her slick gash. He felt her envelop him, her raspberry-pink folds kissing his plum-like cockhead. They were one, at last.

"Yes, music-man. You are home," she said, taking his cock

into her, one hungry inch at a time.

His belly pressed into hers and she whimpered. Their hands twined together and they rocked to a tune as old as time. She kept one foot on the floor and dug the other into the small of his back, riding his length, matching him move for move. He braced her against the door and drove into her over and over, harder and harder.

"Home, home, home. Take me home," he groaned, fucking her faster, deeper.

She urged him on, her body undulating, taking him in and squeezing him until his knees sweat in the creases. His balls lifted, tight, and his cock grew longer and hotter. It hurt, it hurt so good. Fuck . . . fuck . . . fuck. He was going to explode.

"Sebastian! Please . . . please. Just open the door!" A voice begged from the other side of the door.

"Come with me, Lover. Be mine forever. Play for me always," his muse begged, winding her arms around his neck, drawing him back into her. She kissed him as she clung to him, as if without him she would fall. Her voice wove its melody around him, around them both. Everything else faded far, far away.

He reached down, finding her cunt with his thumb, rubbing the apex of her slit until he felt her gather, felt her still, and then come undone all around him. She came, gripping and fluttering—his beautiful muse, his woman, his dream—real. Here. His at last.

"Yesss. I'm coming . . . coming . . . coming!" Sebastian flooded into her, his body giving up his spunk with a force that made him dizzy, as if she'd reached into him and drawn out a piece of his soul along with his orgasm.

They kissed, sharing ragged breath in the decrescendo of their lovemaking.

"I love you." He closed his eyes, resting his lips in the

curve of her neck.

"Always." Her lips moved against his forehead.

"All ways." He promised.

The door finally gave way. Sebastian's manager and assistant spilled into the room along with the theater owner and a groupie or two.

"What the fuck?" someone asked.

The window was closed, locked up tight from the inside.

They'd all heard Sebastian pleading and crying, banging on the door, yelling and playing his violin like a madman. But now, there was no one in the room.

His violin was there, in the middle of the floor, the bow laid neatly across the strings.

Later, some swore they'd seen tendrils of smoke wafting from its fine hairs. Some said they'd heard the faint sound of laughter and music, unearthly music, but no one ever saw Sebastian Lachance ever again.

HAPPY F*&%ING HOLIDAYS

It's a new year.

Big fucking deal.

An enormous, gaudy ball will fall in Times Square. People will party. Numbers will shift on the calendar.

It never changes. Holidays keep coming, one after the other, all year long, all life long. Am I the only person who sees the futility in that?

Don't get me wrong. I'm not immune to the hype. I've gotten caught up in it once or twice— convincing myself this season to be jolly would hold something in it for me of the magic.

But, generally speaking, holidays suck, and I know it.

Christmas is something I get through with gritted teeth and a tight hold on my wallet. Halloween is for children. Valentine's Day is for getting laid, and Thanksgiving? Well, fuck Thanksgiving; it's just a day to kiss ass and eat turkey.

Not an appealing paring.

Other holidays are too stupid to even discuss – St. Paddy's Day? President's Day? Easter? Yeah right - green beer, democracy and people rising from the dead and getting worshiped for it (see Halloween, above).

The only saving grace in Christmas is the presents, and this year I decided to give myself the ultimate gift – I set out to fuck the only woman I've ever been completely, irrationally, helplessly, infatuated with – my mom.

Yeah, I know. I'm a sick and twisted fuck. I never hid that from you, so don't gripe now. Stop reading if you can't handle it. I'll tell you this though; everyone has a secret hidden away, a side nobody else knows about. Here's a rare chance to see one, so stick around if you've got the guts and don't mind digging a stick through your own furtive inner-workings. Discussing these sorts of thing results in self-examination, if only to feel superior in one's own homogenized, morally correct world.

So, yeah, where was I? Right. I wanted to fuck my mom, ring in the New Year, and toss out the old. I figured it'd be a combo present - Christmas, New Year's and Valentine's Days all rolled into one. Maybe Thanksgiving too, if all went well.

I wanted to embrace myself for the first time, to celebrate the new year my way, to say fuck pretense and holly jolly and chestnuts roasting over an open fire, and balloons and fireworks and let's all drink until we puke. Fuck it all. I wanted to make this the holiday of Joe getting what he really wants – himself. I wanted to dig deep down into the meat of me and hug it, like on Arbor Day. They hug trees then right?

So, I invited her out. "Hey mom! We're going out on the town. Doing it up right." "Oh, Joe! That'd be so nice!" Having no clue of my plot, she sounded overjoyed, touched even, that I'd want to spend time with her on such a "special" evening.

I sent her a dress for the occasion, one she'd never buy

for herself. It was my special day, and New Year's Eve, so I bought what I wanted to see her in – a red-hot slip of a thing with a back that dipped all the way to China, and a matching thong. She'd be shocked, but she'd wear it for her darling boy.

"Hot damn, Mom!" I whistled, when I saw her. "You look good enough to eat."

"Ohhh, Joe!" She blushed as ruby as her dress.

I took her to Narsisse Rojo, the perfect place under the circumstances. The opulent nightclub was filled with mirrors, constant reminders of why I was here—me.

We ate fusion, frou-frou concoctions mom cooed over. I sprung for the Cristal, and got her a little drunk. I figured why make my job any harder than it had to be?

While we ate, I thought about women I'd fucked: Boyish Jenny in the 7th grade – my first – a frantic dry hump against an elm tree. Teri the cheerleader, in high school - in my first car, a Dodge Dart with broken springs that added bounce and squeak to the fucks I gave her in the back seat. Joann - a sweet, shy thing with a secret hankering for sucking my dick. She liked it rough, and I liked to see her on her knees, so it worked out just fine. Julia - the one I'd thought I loved, who banged one of her co-workers daily for a year before running off with him on our wedding day. All things considered, I'm grateful she hadn't married me and confessed her indiscretion years into a vaguely unhappy marriage. Imagine how fucked up I'd be then. Things are bad enough.

There were others, some with names I remember, a lot more with names I don't. Hand jobs, blow jobs, rim jobs, fuck-overs and do-overs.

Mom's mouth moved at dinner, but I didn't hear a thing she said. Instead, I heard echoes - a litany of women's voices reminding me why I was here, why this was going to be the year of Joe.

"You bastard! How could you?"

"I hate you!"

"You've got no soul Joe, no heart."

"I loved you, and you fucked my best friend?"

"I never want to see you again."

"Yeah, remember when Todd and I'd come to your office to pick up paychecks? Well, we'd go back to his place after and fuck"

"You're not the marrying kind, Joe."

"You're a child, Joe."

"Go fuck yourself, Joe!"

I could go on, but it's boring. I know. That's why I stopped tuning in, and maybe that's the reason it just continued, with one woman after the other. I used them like towels in the men's room, tossing them on the floor, sometimes walking all over them. I know it sounds like typical man-talk bullshit, but honestly, some of them liked it, for a while anyway.

It would take years more therapy to figure out the why of it, the why of me, and why bother? It's in the past now. Tonight, it's all going to change. I am going to fuck over the best thing that's ever happened to me, and I'll be purged, free to start all over again. Maybe this time I won't make a complete mess of it.

I had thought about trying it a different way. I've never done the hearts and flowers, couple's counseling way. I could find a nice girl, a girl who would beam at me and fix granola in the morning before we did yoga together. We'd hold hands every night and declare, "Today was a great day, and tomorrow is going to be even BETTER."

I could learn to like football and children and the missionary position in our nice family-sized bed. I could even live with the cute little pillows I am sure a woman like this would have everywhere.

I could buy a minivan, and stop jerking off. I could lie in the wet spot.

But, wait a second. That'd all be going against the grain, against the JOE.

I keep needing to remind myself of what I really want and have never been quite in touch with myself enough to admit, much less act upon. It's always been easier to be the cad Joe, the asshole Joe, the Joe with the slick pickup lines in bars that make women melt all the way from their bar stool into my bed, or car, or the nearest bathroom.

I've never been too picky, and that, my friend, is the crux of what's been wrong with Joe until now. While fucking everyone else, I've fucked myself the hardest, the worst, and the most.

I'm going to end all that right here, and right now. Too bad mom is going to hate me afterward.

"Mom, I'm gay," I confess, after the cheese but before the fruit.

AMARANTHINE RAIN

It's raining.

Raindrops compose rhythmic, pitter-patter music as they caress my skin. They leave a brackish tang on my tongue and the scent of springtime in my nose.

Bathed by soothing mist and ambient light, I lie upon warm dirt. Flowers sprout between my fingers, tickling. Newly formed petals nod their colorful heads as they bloom—lilac, indigo, cerulean hues.

I am rain. I am sun. I am earth.

I cannot move.

Vines spiral, serpent-like, around my cock. They squeeze and pulse until I am erect and jerking with lust. I'm flooded with desire, shame, and fear.

My mind, desperately struggling to make sense of things, turns to the Garden of Eden, Heaven, and Hell—concepts once scoffed at. Perhaps I have lost my mind.

Am I dead?

Selfish and aggressive, I'd been a commanding man, wielding my power like a sword, often hurting others self-righteously as I climbed to the top of the heap.

Even as rain and flora begin to work together, stroking

me into an exquisite, surreal orgasm, I feel sure death looms and decide I must be in hell.

"Jack! I can't do it!"

Blinded by pummeling rain, Jack swallowed anger.

Autopilot attached—hating to leave the helm in the storm—Jack fought his way to the bow, where his wife struggled with the tangled emergency parachute.

The storm had struck fast, the seas forming deep valleys their sailboat seemed desperate to cast itself into, suicidal. Any larger and they'd become huge waves, unleashing deadly amounts of energy as seawater crashed down. They'd be crushed unless the chute was in the water to dissipate the ocean's power.

"Move! You're totally useless!" Jack pushed Diane away, ignoring her familiar, wounded expression.

Hell is sunny, yet rain always falls. The sky is cloudless, brilliant blue.

I know I am no longer alone. Untangling myself from sensuous brambles, I walk naked to meet my judge, crushing violets under my feet.

I am surprised to see a woman. She sits as if meditating in the verdant field, her legs folded, palms filling with rain. Her hair is long and brown, her face hidden.

"Diane?"

She is motionless.

I walk endlessly, but she remains out of reach.

Am I dreaming?

Tired, I curl upon the ground, a human snail among the otherworldly vegetation.

I wake to see Diane standing over me, her eyes filled with undeserved love. It hurts to look at it. She shouldn't be here. I weep, tears dissolving in the rain and, for the first time, I suffer regret.

Jack had untangled the chute and lowered it overboard when Diane screamed. The boat had turned its hull to the waves. A wall of water fifty feet high loomed. When it hit, Diane was swept overboard. Jack fell to his knees, desperately clinging to the railing as the sailboat flipped upside down. Had Diane been wearing her lifejacket? He blacked out trying to remember.

Diane's flesh shimmers with rain.

Warm rivulets cascade over me. I don't know if they are her tears or raindrops.

"I'm sorry. About never being home, about the other women, about all the times I yelled at you."

I reach for her, and she shatters at my touch. Shards sparkle as her wreckage mingles with the rain. Soon, I cannot tell her from it. Holding out my hands, I capture wet sharpness. My flesh feels no pain as I bleed, but my heart aches.

I am alone.

Diane has always been my anchor I realize, too late.

Please, come back.

Once, he'd loved her madly.

They'd been high school sweethearts.

She'd given him her cherry after prom, in the back of his dad's Buick Roadmaster. Nothing had ever been sweeter than her shy passion that night, until the day she'd agreed to marry him. He thought he'd never feel happier.

Babies had followed—too soon for Jack's taste—and life rushed by. College, law school, partnerships, and accolades.

Diane mothered the children. Jack traveled, his team of attorneys gobbling up smaller firms until his reigned supreme. If life was survival of the fittest, he had been king.

She returns. Atop me, her legs part, hugging my hips as she opens to me.

We kiss, breath mingling as lips touch. I slide into her slick, coddling warmth and am home. We move languidly in the swirling rain, rolling atop green, plush grass. Velvet soft blades caress us and lupine blossoms around our tangled bodies.

It's so beautiful.

"I love you, Diane. I always have."

"Then stay here with me, Jack. Always."

"Always. Forever." I say words I'd said on our wedding day, making a new promise to make up for the ones I'd broken, meaning it this time.

Jack woke, seeing storm clouds above and dark gray sea all around.

He floated alone in the churning ocean, hugged by his life jacket, unable to move. His head hurt.

"Diane!"

Something nudged his foot, and he was afraid.

I want to go back. I promised.

Heavy rain began to pelt him, and Jack gratefully slipped away from cold, frightening reality back into the lush world where Diane waited.

Are we dying?

We come together—limbs twining like vines, my seed gushing into her vessel—and it seems a resolution has been found and that a new, beautiful life might begin, one with no mistakes, no regrets.

I look into my wife's eyes, hold her hands, and am no longer afraid.

Rain spills from the azure sky, washing away sorrow and taking away pain. Upon an ancient river, we now float coming and coming again as our bodies cling together, eternally pleasured and eternally bound.

"Evermore, Jack . . . mine now," Diane says, pulling me under the waves.

My toes skim pebbles smoothed by time as the water takes me into a dark abyss where violets bloom in currents fed by rain, never ending rain.

THE HOUSE ACROSS THE STREET

The house across the street seemed very old, just the sort of place you would expect to find a historic marker discreetly displayed upon, but I knew it was new construction, despite its antique look. I had watched it being built it from start to finish.

Today, workers had patched together the final touch; a fluffy new lawn now blanketed the space between the house and the fence that enveloped the property in a protective embrace.

Earlier tonight, I had looked at the finished house through a lacy screen of winter-bare tree branches outside my bedroom window. The naked limbs tangled like skeletal lovers and cast twilight shadows onto the pavement below. A chandelier suspended over the home's graceful porch caught fast fading rays of sunlight, splintering them as I watched.

It was beautiful.

Nice houses and people with money were not unusual in my neighborhood, but most people do not rip down a perfectly good Chicago brownstone to build something this interesting. The unique splendor of the new house's design indicated the owner had taste. The speed and quality of the construction told me they also had a lot of money. Old money, I decided. Loving anything hinting at a mystery, I was intrigued.

The lots were tight in this neighborhood near the lake, the buildings squeezed into narrow lots. The builders of the house across the street had made up for the lack of available width by making their structure four stories high with an attic and a basement. Walls of glass supported by stone strips reminded me of those on Gothic cathedrals I had seen and admired in France. A path planted with moss and creeping thyme curved up to a wide set of stairs. The face of each riser had been planted with ivy and tiny flowers, giving the impression of a lavish garden oasis nestled in the close space allowed by the huge house.

The house's windows were darkly reflective. No lights shone from within. So far, this had been typical. Sometimes, I could see my building mirrored but never myself, sitting where I most often sat, in the leather chair behind my desk.

The innermost depths of the house were elusive. It had taken me a while to decide that a single bedroom occupied the turreted attic level. I was enchanted with the place despite my affection for my own charming, but tiny, relic with its whistling plumbing and walls that seeped cold in the winter.

Large pieces of furniture, hulking shapes, had been scattered throughout the house, a few things to a room so far, but I felt certain their appearance meant the elusive owners of the intriguing home would soon materialize. I had enjoyed the delicious anticipation, savoring the vibrantly alive feeling of expectancy —often sweeter than the moment when whatever I had anticipated finally arrived. I had enjoyed my time with the house as it was completed, alone with my fantasies and voyeuristic pleasures. Now, it seemed the end was drawing near. I felt a vague sense of wistfulness. The new people would come. The mystery would be revealed and, I was sure, the reality would be far less exciting than my daydreams had been.

A couple owned the place, I had guessed. They were older. He was retired though he still had a hand in the family business, something glamorous like railroads or shipping. I saw them clearly in my mind's eye. He would be silver haired, tall with a commanding presence, oozing wealth and power, and she would be his perfect foil, slim and elegant, a dark beauty aging flawlessly.

Tonight, as I had watched the last of the sun's light sink into the horizon, I saw that the shades in the house across the street had been opened and the curtains drawn back. Still, though, all I could see inside were the shadowed outlines of the new furniture. It was maddening. The last peachy sliver of the setting sun winked out, leaving only indigo stains in the darkened sky.

Once, a light had appeared in a stairway on the right side of the house's interior. I held my breath as a long, thin shadow slid up the stairs to the opulent bedroom. I saw, for the first time, that the ceiling was domed and swirled with molding painted in shades of gray. The bed was massive and piled high with pillows, covered in silk and velvet. Towering potted trees stood sentinel in each corner, the only witnesses to my prying eyes.

They have a timer I thought as the lights dimmed slowly.

Days ago, I saw a shadowy figure, one with long, spider-like limbs, creeping up the stairs that led to the bedroom. Before I saw an actual person, the drapes that had been swept back to one side of the windows fell over the glass and closed off my view completely. Startled, I pressed closer to my window and, just for a moment, I thought I saw eyes glittering darkly and peering back at me from a small split in the curtains. I blinked, and they were gone.

Now, only the memory kept me company during another sleepless night. There was no sign of movement in the house across the street.

The house, my growing obsession with it, and my fantasies had all stirred me in ways that were sometimes disturbing, sometimes irritating, and sometimes sexual. The night I saw those strange eyes was the first of many I masturbated sitting in my bay window, sprawled naked in my chair, doing it slow, drawing it out, confident no one could see me yet feeling a new thrill at the possibility I was wrong. Maybe someone watched me stroke my cock until I came with equal pleasure, their dark eyes glittering. I had become not only a voyeur, it seemed, but also an exhibitionist.

It had become a game, after the first alarming glimpse of those shadows and odd eyes, trying to get a look at the people who owned the new house across the street.

Last evening, after days of seeing nothing, while I had wrestled with a novel that did not want to wrap itself up and a newly developed problem with insomnia, I finally saw someone again. It had been very late. At first, I had not even noticed the faint light shining in the house across the street. It lit a small hallway in the back of the second floor. I had seen a movement in the soft flood of reddish light. I squinted, reaching for my glasses. Could that be a person sitting there in the hall, I had wondered? Was that blood on the wall or was it all just a shadow's trick?

I had moved closer to my own window and placed my palms flat to the chilled glass as if by moving just a tiny bit nearer I would be able to see more clearly. Would someone sit in the cramped hall in the middle of the night and had I really seen what I'd imagined I had—a person who appeared slouched or even dead? After a few minutes of intent watching, I had begun to doubt it. The faint light was no help. As my eyes adjusted, I could see the dim illumination flickering, like the flame of a candle casting dancing shadows onto the walls. I waited for the person to move for surely I thought, dismissing the idea of a corpse, they would rise to enter the living room or to move down the short hall to what I had decided was the kitchen. I leaned my forehead against the glass. My eyes closed. I swooned, almost giving in to the overwhelming tug of sleep that had crept over me with sudden, grasping fingers. I rubbed the tightness of my temples, flung off my glasses and staggered to my bed.

Why couldn't I sleep? I looked at the clock on my mantel as I passed it. It was 3:08AM. I looked back over my shoulder one more time at the spot in the hall where I had seen the vague shape that might have been a person and thought again of the huddled form, curled around itself, the slow slide down the wall, and the blood red color. The flicker of light had extinguished as if it had never been. I found tortured sleep and dark dreams.

For a while, the lack of activity had caused my interest in the house across the street to fade. Often, when I could not sleep, I read, working my way through the Shakespeare I had missed in college and everything Edgar Allan Poe had ever written. I wrote too, feverishly at times. I worked on my novel, but more and more often, wrote in my journal, my thoughts turning inward. I listened at all hours to jazz and old albums of music from the 20's on the turntable I had found at a garage sale on my block. I had talked with a few neighbors there, casually, thinking it odd no one had anything to say about the strange nonappearance of our street's newest resident.

It was this fact I pondered tonight, deep in the middle of another sleepless night as I looked into the dark, empty windows of the captivating, seemingly empty house across the street. Why was no one else on my block as interested in the place or its mysteries as I was?

When the room I gazed into was suddenly illuminated, I actually cried out in surprise. I muffled the sound with a hand pressed tight to my lips as if whoever had turned the light on would hear me and go away. My brain struggled for a moment with the sudden surreal image of my new neighbors in their bedroom, lit by the glow of a candelabra held aloft by a man who had his back to me. He was tall, slender, with wide shoulders, and a lean waist. His hair was very long, held back in a ponytail that looked like a black snake coiling down his back. Fluttering golden light cast shadows on his face, shielding it from my gaze. He moved to the head of the bed, taking the candelabra's glow with him, placing it on a table there, and bathing the bed in soft shimmers of light. He turned his face and gave me, at last, the outline of his stark profile. I had the impression of a noble nose, full lips, and dark eyes. He reached out, drawing his finger in a slow, lazy path down the long leg of a woman who lay there. The two were definitely not old or anything like the couple I had imagined.

My indrawn breath faded to a gasp as I dragged my gaze from him to her. She had stunning, alabaster skin, slender limbs, and a delicate, lithe little body. She was totally still, reclining on an extravagant pile of pillows. Her flesh was so pale that it seemed to glow in the faint haze of light provided by the candles, the shadows of her body's hills and valleys pronounced. Her sex was smooth, parted, and swollen. I saw her shell-pink slickness. She was a work of living erotic art, a china doll displayed for me in the frame of the house's windows. It was not until she moved again, with writhing, sensuous undulations, that I noticed the thick black cuffs on her tiny ankles and wrists holding her captive and spread-eagled on the bed.

I watched as the man continued to touch her with the tip

of his finger, making his way over her perfect, tiny breasts. He stopped to pinch her rose colored nipples, making her squirm and arch off the bed. I watched, a shameless voyeur, reaching under my shirt and pinching my own nipple until it hurt as he wound her thick black hair in a coil around his arm, bending to her, perhaps calming her with whispers. He turned her head to the side, fanning out her ebony hair—raven ripples on dove–gray silk—before he stepped away.

I watched her, watching him. Her eyes were luminous, inky black pools. Her expression was serene as he tugged what appeared to be black leather gloves onto his hands. He smoothed them over his supple fingers and then turned to the window. His eyes glittered as they met mine.

Oh yes, he saw me. He saw me quite clearly though I stood in complete darkness, my shirt hiked up, my nipple pinched, and my cock squeezed through my jeans. He actually nodded to me and smiled, sending answering chills down my spine as he showed his teeth, gleaming white. Then he reached up and pulled the cable holding the velvet swath of curtains aloft, sending them down in a sweep and closing off my view.

I have sat for a long while now, in the dark, waiting.

I know how it works. Well read, I am a writer and a man who believes in many things others may not. Destiny, fate, and love. Truth and beauty. Dark things in the night.

I left my front door unlatched for him. I know he will come. He read the invitation in my eyes tonight as I watched him, just as surely as I had responded to his unique courtship.

Thinking of what was to come, I shivered in exquisite anticipation.

Much later, he stepped silently out of the shadows that lurk in my brownstone's corners. He stopped as if to display himself for me in a beam of night shimmered moonlight coming from the very window from which I had watched him earlier tonight. He was young, much younger than I had thought, hardly more than a boy really, like me. He wore jeans, a rumpled white shirt, and a scarred leather jacket. A gold cross hung from his neck on a fragile chain. His hair, two raven wings, fell straight and unbound over his shoulders and reached nearly to his waist.

He looked at me with an unearthly stillness, and my breath stopped for the long moment until he spoke.

"You are mine," he said.

I almost fell to my knees, so strong was the pull of him, something raw and tender in his voice as he spoke the words only confirming what we both already knew. My fingers curled behind me, gripping so tightly my nails cut into my palms. I was tossed in the storm of my emotions, frozen there where I stood. Fear and desire mingled to form a heady mixture. It was intoxicating, frightening.

"I can't hurt you," he said, as if he had heard my fearful thoughts quite clearly.

He came closer, so close we could have kissed with only the slightest pursing of our lips.

I heard a sigh, as if from a distance. Was it his? Was it mine? I did not know. This seemed to be a dream. Perhaps it was. Perhaps I had fallen, without knowing it, into a dream that only seemed real. I stood looking at him, shaking with thundering desire. My craving for the full force of him was almost more than I could bear.

Pain and pleasure were both promised in his eyes. Just one touch, my mind screamed.

"Only a taste," he said, his warm breath licking over my mouth.

A tiny flash of lust burst to flame in my heart. I closed my eyes, feeling the burn of it as he slowly lifted his arms, reaching for me, his lips brushing tenderly over mine.

He drew back, pressing his cheek to my throat, resting there against the flutter of my pulse as his hands cradled my head. He smoothed my hair, almost a twin to his own, as he looked at me. Gray eyes, rimmed with thick black lashes, seemed to draw me out of myself and into him. A delicious disorientation danced with my certainty that, if I did not look away, I would be carried downward far from all things logical, no longer caring about anything but this man's touch, this man's pleasure, and all he could give me.

"Not yet, beloved," he said, brushing his fingers over my lips. He pressed his mouth to my jaw.

Yes, this was better. I'd felt a moment of panic when he'd loosened his hold, shifting his weight slightly away from me, as if without him there I would indeed fall into a spiral, unable to stop. I reached for him then, my fingers trembling, clasped behind him, resting in the small of his back as my arms joined the circle of his.

"I love you," I said, at that moment feeling nothing else.

"Not yet, angel," he replied, though in his eyes I saw acceptance.

Clasped close to him, I shivered in his embrace and looked over his shoulder at the bruise-black night sky. It began to rain; silver drops glittered against the paned windows.

He ran his fingers through my hair; I felt the tingle on my scalp even after he had taken them away.

It was overwhelming. My eyes misted as once more love, desire, and fear crashed down upon me. He seemed to know, again, what I was feeling and leaned forward, his luminous eyes filled with love. He lifted a finger, very carefully touching my eyelashes and the tiny lines in my lips. Then, with a startling suddenness, he pulled me close, tight. His strong fingers gripped my arms and he kissed me, hungry this time, opening my mouth with his. I trembled against his cool, silken lips and the unexpected, warm invasion of his tongue. His kiss unnerved me, thrilled me, and left me trembling, wanting more, even as I feared it.

He was patient. He understood. He wooed me sweetly, taking my clothing from me, shedding his own, and laying me down in the crumpled tangle of my crisp cotton sheets. He touched my body with reverent hands.

I shivered as I looked at his pale skin and reached to trail my fingers over his hip, along the planes of his stomach, and over his smooth chest to thread through his wondrous hair.

"Look at me, beloved."

I did, drowning in his gaze. We lay for a long while, pressed flesh to flesh, heart to heart, touching each other with growing need. I knew, finally, with a calming certainty this was no dream as the passion in us quickened our bodies to a fever pitch of lust, drowning out everything else.

"I love you," he said, his tone somber, as if it was a curse laid upon us both.

I felt the words as if he had breathed them into me.

He slid against me, his palms gliding up my back and down again to cup me, fondle me, stroke me, and spread me. He fed me a finger. I wet it for him with slow suckles of my mouth.

I arched against him, my lips parted in a moan against his neck as he penetrated me with the slick digit, hooking it into me deeply. I shuddered.

He calmed me, fingers wrapped around my cock, urging me into a fucking motion, forward and back. Pleasure. Pain. Stunning intensity of feeling.

Never had I felt such complete abandon. Never had I

felt such release. Never had I felt such desire for another's pleasure. He was all things beautiful. I surrendered to him completely.

"Yes, surrender," he said gently.

For a tense moment, I rode the sharp edge of some inner struggle. Then, I turned for him and spread myself on the bed, my fists tangled in the sheets. I shivered when he took his hands from me, and I realized again how much I wanted this, wanted him.

The danger of what we did thrilled me darkly. The newness was dizzying. I was an offering he took, his arms locked to my body as he pulled me back to him. He buried his face in the crook of my shoulder and neck, his lips moving in gentle kisses, his teeth just grazing my willing flesh as he pushed my knees apart with his. He arranged me in a position of supplication, my face pressed into the pillows, my hips raised high for his exploring fingers and roving gaze. I felt the heat from both and groaned, lost completely.

He kneeled between my spread legs. I arched my back, lifting my ass to him like an animal in heat, crying out as he slid home with a single push. He moved slowly at first, carrying me with him past the pain into a place of pleasure unlike any I had ever known. Tortured, loved, beyond redemption, my cries mingled with his, rising and falling in time with his thrusts until he went tense behind me. His hands seemed to push me away as if, in my helpless position, I somehow clung to him.

"Please," I said, in a voice made hoarse with painful longing.

"Yes," he answered, moving over me again and letting me down until my belly was flat on the sheets.

He pushed the long strands of my hair from my back and then rose again behind me, allowing me to fuck the sheets as he gripped my hips.

I turned my head to see him, his head thrown back, the tumble of his own long hair disheveled. It was delirium. He came into me, a flood of wet, his come mingling with my blood. So hot. Pulsing, hurting, giving, taking. I spilled in jetted spurts into the sheets, rubbing the slick of it with my squirming belly, crying out until he stilled his movements. I felt his heartbeat as he lay atop me, turning me to spoon with him after gently slipping free of my body, but leaving something buried deeply.

"My Master," I said, lifting my gaze to his as he held me close.

"Your slave," he whispered with a deep intake of breath.

His gaze was passionate as he turned my head on the pillow and slowly fanned out my hair. His fingers curled under my chin, he kissed me gently, sank his teeth into my neck, and fed.

SOUVENIRS

"I know what you need."

"What?" Morgan's finger marked her spot in the Physics 101 book.

"I said I know what you need." His features were California-surfer-slacker, but his voice was confident, strong.

"Oh? And what's that?" Want and need were sometimes so far apart, she thought. He'd never guess what she wanted, not so soon, but what she needed right now was an A on the Physics test.

He unfolded a piece of paper with a quick snap of his wrist. Numbers, letters. The Physics test answers.

"I just took it. Bound to be the same one for your class." He shrugged.

Their fingers brushed when he passed her the paper. She shivered. "Thanks. I owe you. Big time."

"Go out with me. Tonight." She stood, brushing grass from her jeans. "Okay. Pick me up at the girl's dorm. Eight o'clock."

"Will do." He grinned and her heart did a little flip-flop. Silly, but she couldn't help herself.

It was weird. Jeff had never noticed Morgan before today, not the way he noticed other, prettier girls. She wasn't ugly, just not his type. Her hair was long and brown, worn to hide her face. Her eyes were green he saw when she lifted them from her Physics book. Her tan sweater bagged over what seemed to be an almost boyishly straight figure.

Give her the test answers. He'd heard the voice in his head, as clear as day.

When she'd looked up at him, he could see she liked what she saw. Most girls did.

You can have her. Whatever you want, she'll do it.

He gave her the cheat sheet and asked her out. When it was over, he was convinced it had all been his idea.

There was just something intriguing about Morgan.

That night, she was waiting for him on the steps of the girl's dorm.

"How'd the test go?"

"I aced it!" She grinned and did a little twirl. Would he notice she'd worn a skirt? Maybe wonder what was under it? Guess nothing?

"Of course you did. Thanks to me." His grin was cocky. She liked that. He was used to being in control.

"Yes. Thanks to you." She dipped her gaze, twisting her fingers together nervously, reminding herself to breathe. Jeff was just a guy. Just a big, blond hunk of a guy.

"Movie?" He took her by the hand. They walked toward Main Street. Restaurants, bars, other college kids.

"Sounds perfect."

In the theater, he found seats in the back. She wanted popcorn.

"Popcorn?" he asked.

"I'd love some." It was nice being with someone who knew just what you needed.

Seats in back. Away from people. She wants it, dude.

It was strange, the sudden presence of this new voice, but, so far, it hadn't steered him wrong.

Morgan seemed cuter tonight. The skirt showed off her long, slender legs. She had pale skin, elegant bones. She'd twisted her hair back from an elfin featured face. She really was prettier than he'd thought at first.

Kiss her.

Normally, his style with girls was to take it slow. His dad had taught him to be a gentleman. Sure, he got his fair share of pussy, but he worked his way up to it slowly.

Not with her. Just fucking take it. She'll be grateful.

He returned to his seat, a little unnerved by his thoughts.

Morgan smiled up at him sweetly. Shyly. She trusted him. Liked him. Probably never imagined she'd be on a date with the big man on campus. Maybe he could just take what he wanted. What he really wanted. None of the hand holding, tender bullshit. His cock jerked in his jeans, filling with a rush of blood triggered by overwhelming and sudden lust. *Yeah. Just fucking take her*, he thought. She'd never tell.

The lights went out when he came back with her popcorn.

They watched the previews. Morgan was glad the theater wasn't crowded. No one sat in their row.

The lights dimmed further when the main feature began, and that was when it happened.

Jeff put his hand on her knee, sliding her skirt up her

thigh. "Don't move," he said, his breath hot on her ear. He pushed her legs apart, so far the tendons in her crotch spasmed. "Stay like that."

She was frozen in place. He had big, powerful hands and long fingers. He shoved them into her body with force, tearing her flesh. She gasped, and he bit her earlobe, piercing it with sharp teeth. "Quiet. Hold still or you'll be sorry."

She obeyed, heart pounding, her dry cunt clenching his ramming fingers. Pleasure and pain fought until pleasure won. When she came, her spine curved as her ass lifted off the plush theater seat, her spasming pussy slammed into his spanking palm. "Fuck!" she moaned.

"Yes. Fuck. I'm going to fuck you. But not tonight. Go to the bathroom. Clean up." He stood to let her pass. She ran up the aisle, feeling blood and her own come sliding down her leg.

When she came back, Jeff was gone.

Jesus! He'd never done anything like that before. After, he'd had to leave. Couldn't face her.

He'd been so rough. So mean. He'd hurt her. Bit her, slapped her and used her.

It had been exhilarating. Like nothing he'd ever felt before. He had almost come in his pants like a freshman.

She loved it. You could have even more.

It scared him, in a way. The voice. The feelings. But, by the time he'd reached his dorm, he knew he would see her again.

She didn't tell anyone what had happened at the movies with Jeff, and when he called her cell phone two nights later and told her to meet him at the fountain, she went, even though it was ten o'clock and the campus park was off limits at night.

He watched her from his hiding place behind a thick trunked tree. She looked nervous, hesitating at the point where leaves formed a canopy over the path, plunging it into dark shadows. She'd worn a skirt again, this one shorter. Good. That would make things easier.

She wants it. And now, so did he. The adrenaline was unreal. His veins pulsed with excitement. He had to remind himself to breathe. Somewhere, deep inside, he also felt a thump of dull fear. What if he got caught? This was serious shit. He could go to jail if she cried rape. *She won't. Do it!*

He waited until she'd passed him, and then he stepped out behind her. His feet crunched the gravel.

She turned, her eyes wide and startled. She opened her mouth to speak.

"Shut it. Turn around," he growled the words as he walked closer to her, crowding her, pushing her into a tree trunk.

She hugged the bark, laying her tender looking cheek against its roughness.

He yanked her skirt up and his zipper down, kicking her feet apart with his. Grabbing a handful of her hair, he twisted it, holding her in place. With his other hand, he felt for her hole and found it slick. "You fucking want it." He shoved his cock into her, lifting her to her tiptoes as he fucked her, slamming her pubis into the tree with each thrust. He smelled pine, tart and green. He came so hard, his knees buckled as his teeth took her by the nape, shaking her like an animal in heat, mating.

She never made a sound.

He zipped up, but she stayed where she was, her skirt lifted to expose her bare ass, her arms wrapped around the tree. She was shaking all over.

"Pull your skirt down. Go home."

He walked away, without a backward glance.

Jeff was shaken. Morgan had become some sick obsession with him. He'd not known she was alive until last week, and now all he could think about was tearing into that sweet, young body. His thoughts grew darker, the more time he spent away from her. He imagined violent things that twisted his insides even as they made his dick throb.

He stayed away from her, half-afraid she'd tell someone or go to the cops. He waited, but no knock came at his door.

He tried to go out with other girls. "Are you okay, Jeff? You're so quiet," Brittany asked, pouting.

"I'm fine." He just couldn't stop thinking about Morgan.

He managed to keep away for three days. When he didn't run into her on campus, he went to the girl's dorm. "I'm looking for Morgan. I don't know her last name," he told the girl on duty in the lobby.

"Morgan?" Not on my list. Maybe she moved?"

"Maybe."

He tried her cell. She answered on the first ring.

"I need to see you."

"Are you going to hurt me?" Her voice was whisper soft, childish. Jeff's heart twisted. What the fuck was wrong with him?

Cut her. Make her bleed.

"No. Never again. Just meet me."

They met in the Pentacle Hotel bar. The place was crawling with parents in town for homecoming.

"I got a room," he told her as soon as she walked in.

He hurried her across the lobby and into the elevator.

"But, I thought we were just going to talk, Jeff." She had to skip to keep up with him, and his fingers bruised her arm.

"We are. Privately." His body was drawn tight. He was wired. She could see that.

He closed the door behind them. Room 630—bed turned down and covered in plastic, curtains drawn.

Jeff paced, running a shaky hand through his blond hair.

"You're frightening me," she said, leaning her back into the door. The wood was cold.

"Already? Too bad." His eyes had a new dullness to them. "That means it's going to be a long, scary night for you, Morgan," he said, pulling a wicked looking knife from under the bed pillow.

He came for her.

Red. Crimson. Claret. Burgundy. Rose. Vermillion. Ruby. Magenta. Red. Crimson. Claret. Burgundy. Rose. Vermillion. Ruby. Magenta. The words repeated in his head, like some sick ode to what he'd done to her.

He had never cut deeply enough to kill her, but had marked her body like a map, scoring his name in a dozen places, drawing hearts, knives, and terrible things all over that alabaster skin of hers. By the time he was done fucking her—in every way his newly twisted mind could conceive of—they were both covered in her blood and his semen.

She had cried, in the end. Finally, when she passed out, he arranged her limbs, just so, and fucked her again.

When she woke, he bathed her tenderly, watching her blood turn the bathwater pink.

"I'm sorry. I'm sorry. I'm sorry," he said.

No, you're not.

Morgan traced Jeff's name, a faint scar on her tummy. A souvenir.

She sighed. It hadn't lasted very long. That had been the trouble with all of them so far. The very weakness of mind that made them so easy to bend to her will also made them vulnerable, fragile inside and too soon broken.

Morgan was sad Jeff had killed himself. He'd been the best so far. For a while, she had even thought maybe she'd finally found a permanent playmate, someone as into the games as she was, someone who knew, really knew, just what she needed.

Oh, well. There was always next time.

She drew her knees up to her chest and began to think of new scenarios, new adventures, and new things she might try. The hotel had been the best. She would definitely keep that part, but the movie theater intro was getting a bit old. She'd have to think of something more dangerous and exciting next time.

It was weird. Paul had never noticed Morgan before today.

THE WAY OF A MAN WITH A MAID

London, England, 1851

Ding ding ding! The bell over the bookstore door tinkled. The woman who entered was small, trim, and alone. She wore a large, unfashionable, brown hat, gloves, and a navy blue day dress with a fitted bodice and full skirt.

Finnegan, unpacking a box of dusty old books in the rear of his store, hoped she had coin to spend. Business had been slow. The Great Exhibition had easily lured away his customers. The giant crystal palace, machines that could sew whole coats in minutes, and motor cars were more fascinating than books, even to him. Murphy's Fine Used Books could not compete with 13,000 exhibits, especially when the whole point was to show the rest of the world how superior England was. Everyone in London was there. Everyone, except Finnegan Murphy, and this odd-looking girl.

She did not seem to see him and, with her head turned away, her hat hid her face. Finn watched her slowly draw her gloved fingers over a shelf of leathery spines, books he kept lovingly organized by subject and author. Horticulture, botany, flower arranging.

She moved on, and he glimpsed the tilted corner of her mouth as it lifted into what had to be a smile. She was young, too young to be in a shop unaccompanied unless she was a working girl. A governess perhaps, educated enough to read, though one never knew these days. He'd had gypsies and clowns wander over from the Exhibition and, as different as they were, he had been glad to see paying, book-loving customers.

History, culture, architecture. This girl passed them all by.

Finn's usual, cheery, "Good morning! May I help you find something?" died as only a thought. Instead of speaking, he stepped down an aisle, shielding himself from the girl's view, watching her.

She wiggled long, white fingers free of ladylike, ivory-colored gloves, and removed her ridiculous hat. Her hair was dark and pulled smoothly into a twist at the nape of her neck. The resulting coiled bun looked heavy, and Finn had a vision of her with it loosened. He imagined it reached her waist, and that silken tendrils would flirt with the full breasts held so primly covered by her sensible dress. He imagined nipples as lush as baby-pink fruit, cool on his tongue.

When she turned cat-slanted, amber eyes his way, and their gazes locked, he knew he was lost, though he knew not why. She was exotically pretty, yes. A book lover, obviously. And, those eyes were mesmerizing, true. But, what set her apart from other pretty girls who liked books? Would something justify the violent lust burning through his body as he watched her?

"Forgive me, Miss. I didn't hear you come in," Finn lied, wiping dusty hands on the white smock worn to protect his clothing while handling the books. He rounded the corner, and came face to face with the woman he found so inexplicably arousing.

She was a tiny thing, barely reaching his shoulders. Her hands trembled as she hastily tugged her gloves back onto her fingers. "And, I did not see you, Sir. Quite all right." Her voice was soft, and held a slight quiver.

"May I help you find something? Dickens, Browning, Brontë?"

"No, thank you. Might I just explore?"

"Absolutely. Please, take all the time you would like." Finn escaped, sidestepping away from her, quickly past mystery and science, back to where the crate of books waited to be sorted and shelved.

Good god! What was wrong with him? His breath was ragged. His heart pounded, and his cock had been stiff from the moment she had walked into the bookstore.

He could not stop himself from peering over a row of poetry, watching as she seemed to spy something of interest on a top shelf. Tugging the rolling ladder over, she climbed up and stayed up, curvy hip cocked and leaning into the shelf of books as she read her selection. Finn's mouth went dry when he saw her snug fitting little boots and trim ankles topped with the crisp, white lace edging of her bloomers.

Out of view of the door, and the tantalizing customer, Finn angled his body into the bookcase. A fresh dose of musty leather and papery decay smell hit his nose, increasing his sharp yearning. He did love books. His fingers slid slowly over a buttery soft leather spine. He gripped the book with one hand. Through smock and trousers, ridges of book spines rubbed over his turgid shaft as he pressed himself closer to the bookcase. Baudelaire, Browning, Byron. He watched the girl who still perched atop the ladder, unaware of Finn's raging desire or the battle he fought within himself. A tiny voice urged him to go to her and slide his palms over her shoes, encircle her ankles with his fingers and climb up and under her prim and proper skirt to the bare skin that must lie within all that lace.

He thought of what would happen to him in one of London's squalid prisons if he was jailed for rape and he paled, turning his eyes from her and walking toward the front of the store, via the row she was in. One more look, close up, he told himself. Then, professional courtesy when she departed. Nothing more.

He kept his gaze on the pointy toes of her boots as he sidestepped past, assaulted with a vision of her wearing nothing but those boots. Her skirts brushed his chin, and he stopped in front of the ladder. The scent of lavender and cotton wool mingled with the store's bookish aroma. He had to bite his lip sharply to keep from groaning. His fingers slid over the ladder step to touch the heel of her boot. A thrill shot through him.

About to tear himself away, determined to keep to his plan of ignoring her, he saw what section had so caught her eye, and inspired her to climb the precarious ladder. Kept on the highest shelf in the store were a few slim volumes devoted to erotica, exotica and other literature of a more taboo nature. Highly inappropriate for the average customer, yet sought after by enough that Finn always had a few in the store. This girl was the first person who had ever braved the ladder to get a closer look.

She held *The Way of a Man With a Maid*, so absorbed that she did not even seem to know Finn was there below her, slowly angling his head, trying to catch a glimpse of what lay between her legs.

The perverse book, about the seduction of a young girl by a gentleman who has an erotic torture chamber in his home, contained scenes of rape, mother-daughter incest and extreme sexual suffering. Finn liked its straightforward style and quirky sense of humor, but was shocked to see a woman reading it.

She continued to flip pages, her eyes moving rapidly back and forth. Seemingly unaware of his presence below her, she lifted one booted foot to rest on a higher rung. Finn saw a clean, white petticoat and chemise.

He imagined the thrill of watching her peel off her layers of clothing as she stood on the ladder. She would lean back, naked, her hands touching some of his finest books as he feasted on her. No, she would remove everything but the ankle boots. And she would pull the books down from their shelves, so excited would she be by his expert attention. Finn would help her from the ladder and lean her over a pile of books that would lift her hips to just the right height for a good plowing. No one would enter the store. They would be free to frolic. After, perhaps she would come upstairs to his modest abode and they could read to one another. He had a feeling she might appreciate some of the books in his most private collection.

"Oh!" She'd seen him, lurking below like the worst sort of reprobate. Her foot had come back down to a more modest rung, though she still carried the copy of The Way of a Man With a Maid close to her bosom. Her cheeks held a high flush.

Finn had never seen a lovelier woman. "I, um. Might I be of some assistance?" he asked her, stepping away from the ladder as she came down.

What had come over him? Clearly, he had upset the girl. Acting like a complete degenerate. So unlike him. And, she did not know the worst of it. She would have been horrified to know about his lurid thoughts and desires.

She jammed her hat back atop her head and, unspeaking, made her way to the counter.

Finn gathered his pride and usual professionalism around him and took her coin, wrapping her book in brown paper and tying it with twine. He made no comment over her selection.

Ding ding ding! The bell over the bookstore door tinkled as she left, without a goodbye.

Prudence Smyth's cheeks burned as she hurried down the street, clutching her purchase to her chest.

Hyde Park was busy, the Exhibition in full swing. Throngs lined up to enter the now famed Crystal Palace, happy to pay the shilling for admittance.

Pru joined the crowd, wishing her reticule were large enough to stash her parcel in, just wanting to dispose of the book now that she'd managed to botch things completely at the bookseller's.

She passed by the machines and food stalls, the trees and gardens, until she came to the areas meant just for fun. Here, entertainers walked atop stilted legs, clowns juggled, and little dogs did tricks for the amusement of crowds bored with technological wonders. A tent with its doors folded back in welcome, decorated with images of moons and stars sat off to one side.

"I brought your book," Pru said to the old Romany fortuneteller inside the tent, thrusting the package into her hands.

"And did you get your man too?" She cackled.

"No." Prudence knew now that this whole thing had been ridiculous and just wanted to be done with it all. The things in that book! Shocking. Oddly exciting, true, but nice girls did not read books like that, let alone purchase them. Still, the way she had felt surrounded by all those lovely books, in the presence of such a handsome man, reading about such forbidden things. It had certainly been an adventure, she thought.

"Did you speak with him?"

"No. I was absolutely tongue-tied. I am sure he would have been horrified to know why I was there. As it is, he must have been terribly shocked to see what I purchased."

"Ah. Well now, there you are wrong, Dearie. Had you but the courage to do as I instructed that man would have fallen under your spell. Maybe next time."

"Next time? I do not see how I could ever show my face to him again after the way I acted."

"You'd get farther showing him something more." The gypsy laughed and then narrowed her eyes, leaning forward and lowering her voice as if sharing a secret. "Any more and I charge you, but this I give you for free. Go back. Talk to the man. Say hello or climb that ladder again wearing nothing 'neath your skirts. That'll nab you a husband toot sweet!"

"Thank you." Pru thought she would do no such thing, but she couldn't help but wonder if the woman was right. Maybe if she went back, didn't act like such a ninny, and just said hello, things might go better. Mr. Murphy had seemed interested in her too.

Sabina Fa clucked her tongue as the girl left. These silly chits would never learn. She could take their coin for her advice, but she could not make them heed it. Over and over she would point them in the right directions, tell them exactly what to do (which was usually as simple as putting themselves in the path of their chosen and stating their desire plainly), and over and over, they refused to listen. Now, when she gave someone a feather and said it was magic, or a bit of water in a vial made of red glass, they would say whatever silly words she told them to over their new talisman, complete any ritual. Was it really so hard to speak aloud one's wishes?

Ah well. The lovesick girls did keep her in books she would otherwise never have purchased on her own. Her husband would fall dead of shocked horror if he knew of her tastes, so she had found a way to indulge her baser needs without him being any the wiser. There were so many bookstores in London, so many girls willing to do anything to find true love.

She stashed the book under the mattress in the back of the tent, wishing she had time to read it and indulge in a little afternoon rub, but she already heard the rustling sounds of her next customer outside. Smoothing her skirts, she went to meet them.

Sabina's husband, Elijah, finished with his chores and tired after a long day of hustling outside the tent, settled in their bed. Fishing a meaty hand under the mattress, he dug out the latest book, *The Way of a Man With a Maid*.

His wife would be busy long into the night, and he would have all the time he needed to read and diddle. It really was too bad, he thought, that they could not read it together, but his wife would surely die of shame if she knew he'd discovered her hidden treasures.

Ding ding ding! The bell over the bookstore door tinkled.

The woman who entered was small, trim, and alone. She wore a large, unfashionable, brown hat, gloves, and a navy blue day dress with a fitted bodice and full skirt.

"Hello," Pru said.

Finnegan Murphy smiled. "Hello."

WEATHER GIRL

He wanted to chase storms.
I wanted to fuck him.

Things would have worked out fine if it hadn't been for the final storm.

Seth Johnson was everything my mama had warned me about—sexy, charming, and very married. In my defense, I didn't find out he was married until after we'd fucked the first time. It happened on the job—real professional, I know— but, the thing is, when you're chasing storms, there's this electricity in the air from the lightning, the wind, and the danger. It's easy to get caught up in it and carried away.

I was Dorothy. Seth was the tornado.

The first time I saw Seth, he was on the Weather Channel talking about a hurricane threatening Florida. Around him, trees whipped back and forth, bent nearly in two. Lightning struck a pole near his Jeep, but he was not afraid; he was excited. I swear, a car flew by him at one point and he just grinned. The footage made my nipples hard and my pussy wet, something that hadn't happened in a long time.

Later, I watched him on CNN showing off his latest video and talking about a once in a lifetime opportunity to storm chase one-on-one with him in his chase vehicle as a volunteer with his team. Volunteers could drive their own cars as part of the team, but I was not interested in that. No, I wanted to be sitting next to Mr. six-foot-five, fine as hell, bad ass, storm chaser extraordinaire, Seth.

I interviewed with his assistant, got the job, and the rest is history.

We had each other's clothes off by lunchtime my first day. All morning we sat in his car, listening to the storm reports as he wooed me with talk of F-5 tornados, category five hurricanes, flash floods, baseball-sized hailstones, and lightning strikes.

I couldn't help but notice his cock growing thick and long in his jeans and, apparently, he took note of my nipple issue and horny fidgeting because the next thing I knew, he had one hand in my bra and the other in my pants. Soon, we were fucking like monkeys. I came like a typhoon.

"I'm married," he told me while we sat on the bumper sharing a post-coital cigarette. "It's no problem if you're cool with it."

Honestly? I was cool with his big dick in my hungry cunt and his exciting storm talk, but nice girls don't say things like that, so I just said, "You being married kind of puts a damper on things for me." I could hear my mama clapping. He nodded, taking my rejection well. He didn't fire me and life went on.

Hooked on storm chasing, I justified staying on the job because I really liked it and thought I could get a handle on my lust for Seth.

Everything was fine until the day we got the call to check out a possible F-5 tornado situation. Arcing flashes of blue light had been reported as power lines were hit by strong winds. Soon reports of baby twisters started coming in. We raced closer to the eye of the storm and, when we got about a mile away, it started raining. It was a hot day. The windows of the Jeep steamed up, and we got out.

I stood next to Seth on a fence rail to have a better look. At first, the wind was oddly still but then it kicked up with gale force intensity. Rain whipped my hair into a frenzy, blinding me and tearing at my face. Seth grabbed it, wadded it up, and stuffed it down the back of my shirt. I know he was trying to help, but the storm combined with the way his fingers jerked my hair made my clit tingle. He was wet, his own hair plastered to his skull, every muscle—including the aforementioned huge cock—stood out in stark relief under his soaked clothes. He looked like a pirate, riding out a killer storm on the deck of his ship. All I wanted to do was fuck him, and I probably would have jumped him if the wind hadn't knocked me down.

"Holy shit!" Seth screamed, landing on top on me. "It's a fucking carousel!"

I imagined us fucking, spinning around and around on a carousel, before realizing he meant we'd been trapped in the middle of a rare tornado event where two tornadoes revolve around each other in a carousel-like way. That certainly explained the freakish wind, which literally ripped the shirt off my back.

"Stay down!" His breath was hot on the back of my neck.

I arched up into him like a cat in heat.

The fierce wind swirled around us, raindrops lashed my breasts and the next thing I knew, Seth was jerking my pants down, hauling me up and bending me over the fence rail. Now, I ask you, how could anyone say no under circumstances like that?

Needless to say, (and if you've seen the video, you already know this part) I didn't push him off. No, I spread my legs, and he plowed into me. We surged together as the wind howled and things started flying through the air. Corn was ripped from the fields and, by the time it was over, I had half-moon cuts in my palms from gripping that fence so hard. We were part of the storm, trapped in it, with nothing to do but pray and fuck as the world went wild around us.

We screamed like crazy people when we came. It wasn't until later we found out the whole thing had been taped by CNN's crew. Obviously, they didn't put it on the air, but that didn't stop some yahoo from putting it on the internet.

Seth's wife threatened divorce. I was fired, and here we are.

The good news is I have a new career as the stripping weather girl in Las Vegas and have never been happier.

THE LAST SACRIFICE

The cursed statue had stood in my valley long before even the Druids vanished. It might have crumbled into harmless myth had it not been for the last sacrifice, for all those who came before had walked into death's lair.

I could blame her for everything that happened, but blame is a very human fixation, one they value far too much.

Only time will tell how anyone's story will end, no matter the choices they make. Mine is no different.

I did what I could. My role will have little impact on the outcome. Still, the world is on fire and, though it is not my fault, man will blame me. They always blame the dragon.

The casting of lots decided which girl would become an offering for the basilisk, but never before had the name of a Princess been chosen.

The King and Queen, not having the power to stop the ritual sacrifice, grieved her loss alone for the people of the Haven cheered when the crier read their daughter's name.

Most almost certainly suspected, as I had, that Royal names were not entered into the lottery.

Princess Aerten—unlike her parents and all the girls who had been sacrificed before her—had not shed tears, begged for mercy, or screamed in terror over her fate. "You need not bind me with chains. I go gladly, giving my life so another may live," she said when the Scarlet Knights made to seize her.

Though her words were a dagger to my heart, for I could not imagine a world without her in it, I was there when they took her away—the only one who dared accompany them from the safety of the Haven's protective stone walls into the forest-without-end.

Aerten rode with only a small saddle covering my back and a plain, single-rein bit. Nothing fancy for her, she always said, shooing away the stable lads who thought a Princess's mount should be fitted with a Royal caparison, and a gold bit decorated with fancy bosses.

Today, the knights had seen to it anything of value was left behind. They had not even allowed her a cloak. Her slippered feet curved against the warmth of my ribs, giving my sides a slow caress.

"You are a fine beast, Taran." Her hair had come undone. The long glossy tendrils wound through my mane as her voice tickled my ear.

One of the Scarlet Knights laughed. "Look at 'er, whispering to tha courser like the horse is going to talk right back!"

"Mayhap she thinks it will sprout wings and fly her over the forest-without-end, to a land far, far away," the other knight said.

"Or, grow a unicorn's horn to stab the beastie to death before it can devour her!"

Only the Princess knew how close their jests were to my

reality, for only she knew my secrets, and even she did not know them all.

Aerten did not answer them, though her fingers tangled tighter in my mane, her weight shifting subtly with the rising of her back and the tightening of her thighs. My Princess—proud to the last.

Listening to the knight's taunts, thinking ahead to what waited, I had few regrets, though I felt remorse for my parents' hurt when they discovered I had stacked the lottery to make up for all the years my name had not been entered.

Taran nickered as if reading my troubled thoughts.

"Settle. We will be there soon, and all is well in my heart." I repeated the words like a spell meant to soothe us both, "All is well. All is well."

The Scarlet Knights picked up our pace. As the sun sank behind the Mystic Mountains, we reached a clearing where tall stones curved around the mouth of a ravine, each one carved with ancient symbols that meant nothing to me. The bones of those who had come before, the remains of the dragon's yearly feast, littered the forest floor.

In the center of it all stood a huge statue. Rust and moss covered, almost hidden by vines and brambles. Still the shape of some sort of hound could be made out. From its neck hung chains and manacles. How odd, I thought, to find such a thing here, so far from the Haven. Had it been another occasion, I might have asked the knights what they knew of it, but I had other worries this night.

Before the knights could dismount, I slid from Taran's back. "I would meet the dragon unchained."

"You will be the beast's meal either way." The older of the two knights spoke with confidence belied by the darting of his gaze to the fast sinking sun.

From within the mountain could be heard a deep rumble. The air was acrid and bitter on my tongue. Tendrils of smoke lapped at my feet and flirted with my skirt.

"We canna leave her thus. She is sure to run," the other knight said, though he too remained atop his mount.

"Even if I could make it to the Haven before full night falls, I would not be welcome. Running would mean death. Dinner for the wolven."

"Stand in the circle, by the statue, and I will consider my duty ended. 'Tis the least we can do, but be quick about it. Night comes." His gaze darted to the fast darkening, twilight-blue sky.

I saved myself further torment, avoiding Taran's expressive, equine eyes as I passed his reins to the knight. "Thank you."

Pungent smoke seeped from the fissure in the mountainside. A skull stared blindly up at me from the forest floor. Terror drove me to my knees. Despite my previous intention to go nowhere near the thing, I reached for the statue that had held so many before me as offering for the dragon. Its thorns bit my fingers, sending me to my haunches sucking pinpricks of pain from their tips.

Gloom had overtaken the forest, and creatures crept with skittering claws over dry, fallen leaves in the darkness all around me. I struggled, barely able to resist the urge to run. I knew what terrible things wolven could do. The dragon was a thing of mystery, for no one who ever met it returned to tell any tales. Mayhap a death at its whim would not be as dreadful.

"Come out, come out . . . wherever you are." A hysterical giggle erupted.

"Only you would offer yourself up to a demon, and then goad it with laughter," Taran said, stepping into the clearing.

No matter how many times I saw him first in one form, then the other, it still gave me a jolt. As a stallion, he was midnight black with rippling muscles. As a man, he was tall, and just as powerfully built. Both guises shared the same animated brown eyes and black, silky hair. He wore no clothing and could not have been more beautiful. My heart and my body reacted to him, flooding with warmth and emotions.

"You came back!" I rushed into his arms, wishing I could feel his bare flesh through my gown. I had only seen him naked once before, on a day that now seemed so far away. I had kissed him then, long and slow. Touched him and loved him. Ached for more ever since.

"Of course." He pressed his lips to my forehead.

"Foolish." Burying my nose in the curve of his shoulder, I inhaled his familiar smell—leather, horse, sandalwood soap. Man or beast, I loved him all the same.

"That remains to be seen." He set me gently away from him.

"The dragon will come, and I will die. If you have any sense, you will go now before he comes for me." I entwined my fingers with his to keep myself from giving in to the temptation of his naked body, my lust almost more than I could bear.

"Are you prepared to die?" His voice was gruff.

Shame, and the love I saw in his expressive eyes, prodded me into confessing, "I did it because I was angry. Angry with my parents for continuing the lottery, though surely they could have found a way to stop it. Angry they tried to spare me. Trapped, like all of us, only waiting for the wolven or the dragon to grow strong enough to kill us all. Angry with you for tempting me with things I cannot have. Things you refuse to give me." I closed my eyes, unable to bear the bitter resentment in my heart when I looked at him.

Once, and only once, Taran had held me close, made love

to me and told me his secrets. They were many, and they were shocking, but the only one that truly mattered was his ability to leave the Haven and return to a safe, beautiful place far, far away, occupied by Gods like himself. Many times since, I had asked him to take me there. Many times, he had refused.

"Will you do it now?" I asked, though the question in my heart was, do you love me enough?

"Do you love me?" Aerten had asked, on a day that now seemed so far away.

Above us, the sky was robin's egg blue. Atop lush, green grass, on a blanket upon the meadow, warmed by the sun, danger seemed impossible. "As much as I have ever loved, I love you," My fingers played with her unbound hair.

"Always the riddles. You must have loved many. You are very old."

I teased the tip of her nose with the fuzzy end of a stalk of grass. "You would know no peace if you knew."

She gasped, laughing and punched my arm as she rolled onto her stomach. "That many?"

"Is it not enough that I am here, that I choose to be here with you?" Though I should not have done it, I placed a kiss upon the dimple of her chin.

She sighed, her breath sweet upon my mouth. So innocent, my Princess, so full of youthful yearning for things she thought she lacked. In truth, I had never loved another the way I loved her. She had made many long years of suffering in exile worth the price paid.

"I want . . . more," she said, sliding her fingers under my tunic, cupping her palm over my heart, smoothing the flat of her hand over my belly and under the waist of my trousers. "More," she whispered, her lips moving over mine, her fingers dancing on my skin.

"No," I said as my body betrayed my base desires with flesh that swelled and said 'yes, yes, yes' despite the denial on my lips.

Now, after all that has happened, I have to ask myself if things would have been different had I not given in that day. But, those are worries for another time. My choices have been made, and there is no turning back.

I let lust consume me as I taught her the pleasure to be had with our mouths and our hands, skin touching skin. She was an eager pupil, swollen and wet with her own desire under my fingers and tongue.

Under the summer afternoon sky, I made love to her and found peace unlike any I had felt since being sent to the Haven. I forgot everything but her, and I fell in love, deep and true.

Drunk on lust, I let down my guard. Though stories were coming more frequently of wolven striking people in full daylight, I was not prepared. Rubbing myself between the squeeze of her slippery thighs, arm wrapped around her curvy hip, fingers buried in her sex, I did not see them coming until they were upon us. Snarling teeth snapped at empty clothing. Their confusion over finding only cloth in their muzzles is what saved us. As the enraged wolven shredded our clothes, I changed from man to horse to save her. I did it without thought, breaking one of the only rules the Gods had given me, leading me into telling her afterwards almost all of my secrets, giving her my trust as well as my heart.

"Will you do it now?" she asked, the question in her eyes, 'do you love me enough?'

"I should never have told you I can leave the Haven."

She came to where I sat, kneeling on the ground at my feet, clasping my tightly tucked fingers in her own. "Take me to your true home. Save me from the dragon!" "They've never failed to give him his due. If you leave now, what then?" The bitter taste of shame twisted my mouth. Until now, I had given no thought to my duty to the Haven's inhabitants.

"Maybe they will not realize we have gone, and no one will have to die at all this year."

I shook my head. "I must remain."

"You said you could go!"

"Not at my will or yours."

"More riddles. If you do not leave, we both shall die." She rose from her knees, brushing the dirt from her gown.

"I will do anything possible to save you, but I cannot take you away." My duty was to watch over her people, but my heart ached at my failure to give her that which she desired most. Even if I prevented her death now, I knew not where I could keep her safe. I could not take her to my home or hers. She had nowhere to go.

"If you cannot save me, then love me, Taran. Love me before I die. Just once. Give in to it. Just once."

I held out my hand to her and, may the Gods help us all, there was no going back.

I ran to him before he changed his mind. Into his arms I came, standing between the spread of his thighs as his fingers worked the tiny buttons of my dress. I dared not speak, lifting my arms to help him pull each piece of cloth from my trembling body.

My emotions were beaches, like the ones he had described, with opposing shores. The moon of my desire fought my innocence for the water's caress.

"Still, calm," Taran said.

My fingers trembled, but his were sure as he rolled me to rest like the sacrifice I was, prone upon the slab of stone.

All around us, smoke swirled, but even the fear faded when we touched. Lying beside me, he traced my skin with gentle fingers, kissing me until I spread my legs, eagerly.

Against my hip, I felt the press of him, long and hard. I had only seen horses mating. Hiding behind the stable, thrilled by the forbidden sights and sounds as the grooms had led an eager stallion to a mare, I had been horrified and excited. The great male horse had reared and pranced, snorting as his mate turned her rump to him, tossing her black mane. Out of the sheath under the steed's belly shot a tube of flesh, easily as long as my arm and as thick as a small tree. This he plunged into his mate, pawing the air above her head, biting at her neck in his frenzy. When he was finished, though the grooms tried to prevent it, his glistening appendage slid from the mare and sent his seed gushing over the hay in a torrent.

Now, as I felt the press of his hard flesh on mine, and my thoughts brought me back to that memory, excitement coursed through me. Though I was frightened, I knew he was not as large as the horse had been, despite his dual nature. I turned slightly so I could take it in my hand, and knew at once that I had done the right thing for he sighed, his muscular thighs quivering as I ran my hand over the velvet surface. Like steel beneath silk he was. I grew drunk on a power I might never have the chance to use again. Already, my mind conjured memories of his taste on my tongue, his hands on my flesh. This time, I knew there would be more. I would have it all.

It was as my mother had told me, when I had come of age as a maiden. "You will know what to do. Your body will show you the way to your man's pleasure." She had not spoken of the delight I might find, but I felt it now.

I thought again of the stallion and mare; the flesh between my legs tingled with want. The buds of my breasts rose to peaks begging for the warm suckle of his mouth. Each pull of his lips, each scrape of his teeth against my sensitive flesh sent me higher, closer and closer to something wondrous. "Show me," I begged, knowing the wisdom in my mother's words as my legs parted of their own accord and he moved between them.

His answer was to slide into me, slowly but firmly. Pain was a dull sword in my belly, soothed by the sweet rubbing of our bodies as he moved within me. Soon, I knew only fullness and beauty, and once again I climbed to that place he had shown me before that I had longed for since. It was love, I thought as I came undone with the exquisiteness of our joining. True love.

After, he held me close, kissing the sore place between my thighs, wiping the droplets of blood away that I had shed with my chemise and virginity.

Had we been able to stay just like that, until our heads cleared, maybe we would have had a chance, but just like on the day the wolven attacked, we were enraptured by one another, and taken completely by surprise.

A voice rang out, "Virgin blood, upon the sacred stone, taken by one charged with doing the humans no harm!"

Aerten screamed. I pushed her behind me as a giant of a man, clad from head to toe in armor the likes of which I had never seen, appeared in the smoke-filled clearing. Expecting a terrible dragon, my confused mind could not reconcile this man's presence or his strange words.

Flame shot from the dragon's lair and the beast slithered into the clearing at last—every bit as fearsome as I had imagined him. Covered in emerald scales like battle shields sharp enough to flay a man alive, with jack-o-lantern teeth filling a jawbone so full it could not close, and orange eyes that burned like the fires of Hades; he was the stuff of nightmares.

Never had I been more stunned when the dragon roared, "Aye, the terms have been met. Be gone!"

"The sacrifice is still mine!" The warrior's growl sent bats flying from the trees. In the forest, wolven howled.

His metal-gauntleted hand knocked me aside as easily as a man swatting a fly. Catching Aerten's arm, he lifted her clear from her feet, hauling her up to eye level, scowling through the slit in his helm as his gaze met hers, just before she fainted. Tossing her over his shoulder, he stepped into the forest's darkness. They were gone before I could even find my feet.

"You cannot track him down low," the dragon said. The harshness had gone from his voice and the fire had faded from his eyes.

"Who is he?"

"Lord Wulfgar, ruler of the wolven. Do you know the legend?"

"No."

"Wulfgar was a man once, a fierce and arrogant warrior. His ego caught the attention of the Gods, who sent down their finest fighter, challenging him to a fight, promising eternal life and rule of the wolven if he could best their champion."

"He lost?"

"No!" the dragon roared. "He tricked the God's champion, defeating him, but earning their anger. They gave him eternal life as promised, but as a statue of iron, alive only once a year unless his spell was broken."

"For how long?" If he turned back into iron, it was only a matter of waiting, unless he fed Aerten to the wolven before he went.

"You and the sacrifice are responsible for breaking the spell! Now, he will bring war to your Gods and her people. If he wins, he gains true eternal life."

For the first time, I noticed the statue that had stood in the clearing had vanished.

"Why now? Why Aerten?" *Why on my watch*, I wanted to scream.

The dragon sighed. Wisps of smoke curled from his snout. "I am old, I am tired, and I am very, very hungry. Go now. They headed for the top of the mountain."

"Can I defeat him?"

"In truth, you would be best served carrying a warning to her people and to the Gods. Sacrificing her to save many is the wise, but more difficult choice."

The dragon was right. It was all I had waited for, all these years. My one true purpose—to alert the Gods should war threaten the humans. I had to go home.

I woke with an aching head and a heart torn asunder. Upside down, hanging over the warrior's enormous shoulder, I knew Taran was dead for he would not have let the beastly man take me without a fight had he lived.

Up and up we climbed, into the rocks and ruts of the mountainside. Was this my penalty for being such a foolish girl, willing to risk everything to taste a bit of life, a morsel of freedom, forbidden things?

When I stacked the lottery stones, I had been prepared to die in the dragon's valley. Anything to force Taran to take me away with him. Now, I would give anything to take it all back, to save Taran, even the pleasure found beneath him. How thoughtless I had been. How selfish.

My captor stopped his climb, tossing me to the ground

where I huddled, naked and afraid.

I expected to see sharp claws when he stripped off metal gauntlets and huge teeth in a monster's maw when he removed his helm. Instead, he revealed strong, capable looking hands and a handsome face. In the Haven, he would have set any young girl's heart aflutter with his good looks and mine was no different. My cheeks flushed hot.

"Not what you anticipated?" He smiled, showing perfectly normal, white teeth.

"You, and indeed this entire night, have held naught but surprises." My fingers closed on a stone. I hid it behind my back, lifting my knees, shielding my body from his devouring gaze with my hair, which fell in tangles around me.

"What use will rumination on the past do? Better to move forward, into the now we find ourselves in." His blue eyes twinkled.

Handsome, well spoken, and a philosopher? I could not reconcile the riddle of him and was more than a little disturbed by my attraction to him. "What now then?"

We had come to a place on the mountain where the trees were thin and stubby, the landscape made up of black flintstone, boulders and dirt. I was reminded of my father as I watched him perch a mail-covered foot upon a large rock and survey the forest below us as a King would his kingdom. The howls of the wolven had grown closer, and now seemed to come from all sides.

"I could eat you, or fuck you," he said, the growl in his voice matching the hunger in his words.

I shivered, wrapping my arms about myself. "I am very thin, surely not fit for a meal."

"Pity. Skinny and no longer virgin." His gaze dropped, seeming to see right through the protective veil of my hair.

"Hardly worth your time." I inched away from him.

"Still, it has been an entire year since I felt the pleasures to be had in the arms of a wet, willing woman." He took a step closer to me and, despite my fear, I felt myself begin to respond to him.

"I would hardly be called willing."

"I watched you fucking him. Touch you just right and you'll be willing all right, as willing as they come." He reached out and brushed the hair back from my cheek, and my nipples hardened and proved his words true. "Fucked by a man who knows a few things your tender young lover hasn't learned yet. Things about what women really want."

What could I say in reply? I had become a wanton in Taran's arms, and the thought of doing the same with the powerful and handsome stranger had indeed made my body tingle, setting my mind to visions of things I might be made to do with him.

"There is to be a war. The only thing you need concern yourself with now is whether you will be my Queen and bed-mate, or food for my minions. What shall you choose?"

My fingers itched to throw the stone at his arrogant head. "Our Haven is not worth a war."

"While your people busied themselves behind their walls, they have been watched keenly and closely by those who put them there to start with. The Gods are the ones bringing the war. I only defend my own. As my Queen, you will become a Goddess when we defeat the Gods."

"I see no God in you!"

"I see a frightened girl who has a choice before her! Queen and willing little fuckmate or meal to the wolven?" he growled.

The wind screamed, and from above us came a great flurry of sound, unlike anything I had ever heard. Falling from the night sky came an extraordinary beast—an enormous, black, winged horse whose flailing hooves struck my captor knocking him to the ground.

The Pegasus horse landed in the clearing. His nostrils flared. He snorted, sending a puff of breath over my fingers that stayed lifted in fear until his familiar, equine gaze found mine and he came to a kneel before me.

"Taran!" My man of mystery and riddles had kept this last secret to himself.

Behind him, the stricken warrior came to with a mighty roar. I jumped upon Taran's back, holding tight to his mane as he flew into the night.

Below us, the warrior bellowed, kicking up flintstones that sparked. The wind caught showers of glowing orange embers, sending them dancing over the treetops below us, setting the rain-parched forest aflame like kindling wood. Fire raced down the mountainside.

The wind and smoke teared my eyes, and I gave thanks to the Gods for Taran. I would never tell him about the choice I had been about to make when I thought all had been lost, or of my shameless fantasies about my captor.

"Some things, a woman must bear for her man," my mother had taught me and, in this, I believed she was right.

My Princess was finally getting her wish—I am taking her home.

Cursed, never again to know a man's pleasures, trapped forever more in the form of a winged horse; I had made difficult choices this night. Yet, it was far from over. There would be thorny questions to answer, decisions to atone for, and a war to fight.

What is man's greatest strength? I cannot answer. Love is mine. I only hope it is enough for my Princess when I can finally tell her everything.

PEARLS FOR CHRISTMAS

Christmas Eve

In the hotel's public restroom, John washed his hands, avoiding his reflection in the mirror over the sink. He knew his age showed in the receding hairline, the wrinkling around his eyes, and his soft middle-aged body. It was too late to do anything about all that now. He wondered if Diane would still be able to see the boy he once was.

He remembered her laughing blue eyes, her cheerleader's legs, and knew that no matter what time had done to her, he would still find her beautiful. One never really gets over their first love.

Settling again on a barstool, he ordered another beer, checking his watch. She'd be here soon.

Looking around, he thought he'd never seen such a group of sad men in his life, all of them alone on Christmas Eve, nowhere to go but a bar for a skimpy buffet and the companionship of others in the same boat. Expressions morose, most sat alone, toying with their drinks to the faint strains of Jingle Bells.

Meeting at the airport would have been worse, all those tearful reunions, frantic people rushing through security trying to get to the trees, the presents, the waiting families. Her hotel had been John's idea, the thought of the room upstairs pushed away but titillating all the same. At least they'd be away from all that other crap. His first suggestion had been atop the Sear's Tower, but she'd said she didn't think she was quite ready for a "Sleepless in Seattle" type thing. They'd not seen one another for thirty years, so maybe she was right.

"John?" The soft voice startled him from his thoughts.

And there she was—Diane, grown up, professional looking in her black coat and suit, her hair faded to a soft gold, her eyes still startling blue.

"Diane," he said, rising.

There was an awkward moment, when neither seemed to know whether to embrace or shake hands, and then she was in his arms. She smelled of coconut shampoo, and he thought of the beach even as he felt the damp of melting Chicago snow on her coat.

"I knew it was you, even from the back," she said.

"You too. You haven't changed."

They stood looking at one another until John remembered his manners and offered her a drink and a stool.

"You know, my flight was so long, and this week has been nutty, what with the holidays and all. Would you mind if we went up to my room and ordered room service? I'd love to get these heels off," she said. Her eyes held no guile, no seduction.

"Absolutely! Have you checked in?"

"Yeah, I got a suite. Perks of being a business regular," she said, laughing.

They walked through the busy lobby, and Diane drew looks, the way a tall, well-dressed woman always does. He felt oddly proud, imagining she belonged to him in some way. He sucked in his stomach, his head raised higher. He'd never forgotten the way it felt having her at his side. In junior high, he'd been popular, student council president and the captain of the junior varsity football team. She'd been head cheerleader, but somehow he had always felt blessed the day Diane Prescott had agreed to wear his JV jacket. She'd made him better, more than he was alone.

Riding up in the elevator, he thought about all the years past, the years apart, and realized that each minute spent with her today was like a pearl on a strand, a very short strand. No matter what happened, he wanted to savor each moment.

The suite was nice, the views of the city spectacular, but he barely noticed. He watched instead as Diane sat on the edge of the bed, slipping a finger into the back of each shoe, kicking them off and wiggling her toes in their black nylons.

He perched on the bedside chair, close enough to touch her, but keeping his hands to himself.

"I couldn't believe it when you emailed," she said.

"I couldn't believe it when I saw that picture in Skyline. After all these years, there you were."

"I've worked for Skyways for years, and it's the first time they ever did an article on marketing. Weird how you happened to fly that month and saw it!"

"Like it was meant to be. I usually fly United."

"Yeah, maybe so."

They fell into silence again. All the years they'd been apart seemed to swell between them. He wanted to ask questions, but feared the answers. He thought again of the strand of pearls, each bead a moment in time they could share, each one a gift on its own. The rest didn't matter.

"I . . . well, you really are just the same, Diane," he said, feeling so much—confusion, longing, love. He wondered if she saw it in his eyes.

She laughed, reaching for his hand. "I am forty-five,

John, hardly the same."

How could such a simple thing as this woman's hand in his stall his heart, make him tremble, leave him at a loss for words? He couldn't let go and felt her shiver as he swept his thumb over her fingers.

"To me, you'll always be fifteen, Diane." Jesus, he thought. That was lame. Of course he didn't mean she was childish. He only meant she was the same girl he'd fallen in love with. He fretted until she smiled and, once more, everything felt good again.

She squeezed his fingers and he stood, sliding his hand under her hair, his fingers dipping into the furrow of her nape. She sighed as if surrendering, her cheek to his belly, her arms wrapping around him, pulling him down.

It was awkward, sudden. He was on top of her, crushing her. Their buttons snagged, their teeth bumped, their hands fumbled, but the first kiss melted all that away. Their bodies seemed to find the way, fitting like puzzle pieces. He lifted her skirt, finding the stockings stopped at the top of her thighs. Her skin was soft. Her panties silky. He hooked his fingers under the crotch, and pushing them aside, buried two fingers in her.

Diane whimpered, spreading her legs, fumbling for his belt. He helped her, undoing his fly, pushing clothing out of the way, sliding into her as if they'd done this many times. She wrapped her legs around him, and they moved together slowly.

He lifted himself above her, palms to the mattress, and she wrapped her fingers around his tie, pulling him closer. He tried to memorize each sigh, every little sound she made, and the way her body seemed to shelter him within its curves the way no other woman's ever had. She never closed her eyes and, in the end, neither did he; he flooded into her with a groan, eyes wide open.

After, he took her with his mouth, tasting himself in her folds, marveling that he'd never done such a thing before, not right after sex, feeling closer to her for doing it, darting his tongue over her excited flesh until she clenched his hair and cried out his name in her pleasure.

Much later, they lay wrapped together. He folded his arms around her, giving her head a place to rest in the cradle of his shoulder. His fingers softly skimmed her flesh, finding a belly that was soft, marks there telling him she'd had children. He touched the ruffle of her lashes, the tuft of hair between her legs, and the slick wet they'd made there together, clinging to her inner thighs like honey.

"I can't," she said, as if he'd asked her a question.

"I know." He closed his eyes, thinking again of the pearls, almost feeling them pop off the strand of time, one by one, nearing the end of the line. He couldn't do this. He couldn't just let her go again, but he didn't say anything more.

"It's just," she started, stopped by his finger on her lips.

"Don't. Really. It's okay," he lied.

She quieted, sighing deeply, closing her eyes and snuggling closer to him under the covers. They'd long since abandoned their clothing, having made love three times, using the chair, the shower and the bed. Her flesh now felt as familiar to him as his own.

She fell asleep, and he drifted off thinking of all the times they'd touched when they were kids, all the petting on cold bleachers after games, sheltered by his varsity jacket, nowhere else to go. He remembered the day he'd come in his pants, her hand just stroking him through his jeans as they kissed. They'd been so innocent then. They'd thought there would be time, so much time, neither counting on factories closing, parents having to move away, lost postcards, lost dreams.

They slept until he woke, startled by the sunlight streaming through the window. It was Christmas morning. He had to go home.

Christmas Day

The house was quiet. The tree was decorated, presents in a pile underneath. He saw Santa had filled the stockings hanging from the mantel – candy canes and stuffed animals. In the kitchen, the turkey waited, already in its roasting pan, tucked among the other goodies in the refrigerator.

John wandered the rooms like a thief as if sleepwalking in his own house. He kissed his kids, tucking Jimmy back in, retrieving Janie's Dora doll and laying it on her pillow. They'd be up soon.

In his bedroom, it was dark. Susan had pulled the shades and the morning sunlight barely made a dent through their opaque surfaces.

She stirred in her sleep, tossing the covers from her shoulders. He saw a red spaghetti strap and knew she'd worn the nightgown she always wore when she wanted him to make love to her.

"John?" she said, her voice thick with sleep.

He sat on the edge of the bed, unable to meet her eye. How many times had he made love to this woman? How many times had he told her he loved her?

"Hey, you," he said, lamely.

"Where were you? I was so worried."

He almost heard the pop of that final pearl, rolling under his bed, the one that said it's now or never, John. Tell her the truth or hide and lie to her some more.

Her eyes searched his, real worry creeping in for the first time.

"John?" Her fingers lifted to curl over her heart as if protecting it from a blow she knew was coming.

He thought of Diane, his only true love. He thought of his wife, whom he'd never strayed from before, whom he'd promised to love and cherish until death. He thought of the sleeping children they'd wanted so badly and had such a hard time creating together. He thought of the tree, the presents, and the turkey.

Burying his face in his hands, he said, "Susan, I've got something to tell you."

Merry fucking Christmas, he thought, and then he began.

I LIKE TO WATCH

I like to watch other men fuck my wife. We've been doing it for years. It turns us on.

Back when it started, I told her, "I'm involved in everything or we don't do it."

She'd agreed; she'd been the one to bring it up. "I want to fuck other people, but I want you there too."

It seemed too good to be true. "What if I want to have sex with other women?"

"That's the idea. We do whatever we want, but always come home and fuck our brains out after."

I said yes.

At first we went to swinger's parties, but weren't comfortable in more aggressive settings. The lifestyle resort was a disaster too. We discovered, quite by accident, hotel bars were fantastic for meeting men ready to fuck another man's wife.

I would have preferred to switch it up. Though we'd agreed the sex was to be anything goes, my wife discovered she couldn't deal with another woman in the equation. We tried several times before turning exclusively to men. I discovered the pleasure of watching because of the first one.

Young, rough around the edges, he was a blue-eyed cowboy out of place in the downtown Atlanta hotel bar. He was killing time until his room was ready, and desperately wanted a shower. We told him about the whirlpool as big as a pond in our suite.

He knew the score. "One thing. I'm not into dudes. I'll fuck your wife all night long, but you don't do anything but watch. Try anything weird and I'm gone," he said in the elevator on the way up.

We agreed, eager after months of thwarted attempts. If it turned out one of us couldn't handle it, we had only to say the word we'd agreed on, and it would be over.

He stripped, winking at me when he settled into the steaming tub my wife prepared. He was a cocky little fucker, sexy as hell; even I could see it.

My wife captured my hand and pulled it under her short skirt. She was slick with excitement, swollen and aroused.

I nudged her toward the cowboy.

"I love you," she whispered before she went to him.

I sat on a chair facing the tub, nursing a scotch.

My wife took off her clothes, slow like the cowboy had, and joined him in the tub. She added bubble bath first, letting the cowboy see her from every angle. His cock stiffened and bobbed on top of the water. She was shy, and a little giggly, until he began to stroke it. He touched himself as if he was alone, spreading his thighs, taking his time about it. This was the first explicitly sexual move anyone had made, and it seemed to take everyone but the cowboy by surprise.

I sat up higher in my chair, leaning forward. My wife's mouth made a fuckable bull's-eye of surprise as she took him in hand and stroke-sucked him into an orgasm that came quick and hard, leaving them both panting, the floor covered in soapy water.

He was young, and had not lied when he said he could

fuck her all night.

At one point he said, "You can jerk off, dude, if you want to."

I wanted to, but I didn't. No. I liked to watch, I had discovered. My cock throbbed in time with the cowboy stud's pumping ass as he shot his load into my slutty little wife. I liked it. A lot. I loved watching her cum because of a stranger we'd picked up in a bar. I loved knowing he would go home, and we would fuck like we'd never fucked before because we had shared this. I loved the idea of my cock entering her cum-slick holes after he'd had his fill of her. It was like watching live porno starring someone I fucked regularly.

In the morning, we showered, ate, and he left. We never got his last name. My wife and I made love until checkout time on Sunday.

It was the beginning.

We did it almost every Saturday night after that. Our private sex life was never better.

Tonight was pretty much the same, except it was a Tuesday. My wife had called and told me that she had to work late. Nothing unusual lately, though I did find it odd that the job, that had always been

9:00 to 5:00, suddenly demanded so much overtime. Uneasy, maybe even a bit suspicious, I followed her. She left her office at 5:00 on the dot and met him in a hotel bar—not one we'd been to together.

She knew him. I could tell by the way they said hello, the way they touched.

They checked into room 1408.

I waited until the room service chick left, counting on my wife's lover opening the door when I knocked, assuming something had been forgotten. He did, and I was in, my gun drawn.

"Mike!" Of course, Janice was startled. "It's not what you think!"

I laughed. Of course it was. She was naked, in bed, sheets pulled up under her chin. He was wearing a white robe.

He sat next to her as I brandished the pistol. "She said you like to watch!"

"Oh? My invitation to the party just got lost in the mail? Sorry for the delay then. Carry on." I swept the gun over the bed, like a game show host awarding a prize.

They were quiet. Guilty. Afraid.

"Fuck her," I said.

They stared.

"Fuck!"

They reached for one another tentatively.

"Make it good," I said.

I thought maybe he'd have a hard time getting it up, but he didn't. She loosened up too once he'd had his tongue buried in her for a while.

It was different, my emotions made me edgy, not aroused. My cock didn't respond until he buried his in her. I liked that he fucked her, and hated it too.

I watched my wife cum, fingers buried between her splayed legs as her lover plowed into her from behind.

I put the gun down. It wasn't loaded anyway.

When I reached for them, they welcomed me, pulling my clothes off, falling upon me. He hadn't come yet and was so hard. When he guided my mouth to his pussy-slick cock, I sucked it while Janice licked and suckled mine, fingering herself into a bucking frenzy. She wanted more. Excited, hopped up on the adrenaline of it all, I thought then only of the pleasure to be had.

We sandwiched her between us, aroused cocks rubbing together through the thin skin between her pussy and her ass. Later, I filled his enthusiastic mouth with my cum while Janice watched. I don't know if she came too, but my orgasm held the power of years of pent up desires, never even realized until tonight, and now playing out so perfectly.

It was hotter than anything I'd ever fantasized about, watching my wife fuck the endless stream of sexy men, unable to participate. I had nothing else to lose, and fucked them both in ways I hadn't even dreamed about. I loved every minute of it. I lost count of the times I came, or watched someone else cum.

After, he left.

Janice and I quietly went about the routine morning-after business of cleaning up, eating, recovering.

I don't know what I am going to do about her, or our fucked-up marriage.

I still have the gun.

THE QUIET CAR

Her eyes are closed. I imagine they are brown, though their color is of no concern to me. Part of the game is trying to piece these things together. When she wakes, I will know and be satisfied.

The small hills of her breasts rise and fall as she breathes. I ache to reach out and touch her hands, curled together like wounded birds in her lap. "It's okay," I would tell her as my fingers cover hers. "I'm watching over you."

In her sleep, her eyelashes flutter and her knees part. It is so hard to hold your legs together once sleep overtakes you.

My gaze travels up to her crotch, covered in sensible wool trousers. She is wearing white cotton panties, I decide. They cover an abundant thicket of pubic hair—black, though the hair on her head is bleached blond.

I admire the smooth, fair skin visible where her blouse falls away from her throat as I tilt my head, trying to see between the navy fabric and flesh. No hint of a bra strap. White, I envision, to match her panties. Old-fashioned and sensible, the way this woman appears to me, with her penny loafers and black leather COACH bag. She wears a delicate gold chain around her neck. Cradled in the hollow of her collarbones, it pulses rhythmically.

Around us, others go about the business of getting to work. There isn't an empty seat on the rush-hour train into Chicago. I had to arrive early to get my coveted spot in the Quiet Car. There are only two seats facing the rest of the passengers. Riding backward is a small price to pay for the best view of my fellow commuters, who all face forward and sit side-by-side.

Every day, someone new sits across from me. "Excuse me. Sorry," they usually say, as they take the only seat left, the one that requires them to sit face to face with a stranger, forcing them to shift their legs to avoid bumping mine.

"No problem," I always reply. I am pleased to make room for all of them. Old, young, male or female. They all hold their own mysteries, their own allure.

Though I could sit in a backward facing seat on other cars, I prefer the Quiet Car. Here, silence is mandatory. This encourages riders to sink into their own worlds instead of chattering to one another, or clicking away on laptops that hide so much of what I wish to see. I do not mind the new electronic reading devices. They are as small as the fancy cellular phones so many carry now, and do not obstruct my view. Sometimes, I catch book titles, gaining new clues about the day's subject. You would be surprised at who is covertly reading trashy romance novels or guides to bomb building, though I rarely am.

When someone unfurls the day's newspaper, or unpacks a bag of knitting, my gratification is minimized along with my view, though not always. Sometimes, I find pleasure in the smallest things— plump, young toes in flip-flops in the summertime, nails painted garish colors; a minute track of stubble on an otherwise smooth calf, or a glimpse of ankle between sock and shoe.

The woman across from me stirs as the train makes our first stop. Her eyes open. Brown, as suspected. I look away, through the dingy window to the murky view outside where familiar faces smile from the platform, waving goodbye to people who are not me.

I have been commuting by train for eight months, long enough to recognize the kiss-and-runs, the two chatty old ladies who always ignore the Quiet Car signs, and the men who seem to wear the same suit and tie day in and day out. There is the elderly Asian woman who never looks anyone in the eye, and the gregarious dwarf who seems to know everyone else on the train. Though I have noted their presence, like cogs in a mutually beneficial wheel, I have discouraged all from taking the seat across from me. A loud cough usually does it; no one wants to sit by someone coming down with a cold. I quiet once the regulars take their seats, holding out for someone new and unexplored. Like this woman, today, whom I have never seen.

Her eyes drift closed when the train lurches forward once more. Something about the rocking motion seems to lull so many into a morning nap, even those equipped with travel mugs filled with coffee.

In her bag is a stainless water bottle, with no visible logo, and a book she does not read. To Kill a Mockingbird. Classic, just like her. No surprises there. Notebooks and papers fill the rest of the viewable space inside her purse. She works a day-job and attends a University at night, studying writing. Does she long to tell the world her stories? No, I decide. She isn't curious enough about the people around her to be a writer. She is studying literature. Someday, she hopes to obtain a teaching position and a mate. She wears no ring. I do not presume her sexual orientation, though I hope she is not gay. I prefer to indulge in a fantasy of what might happen should our eyes meet and love blossom instantly, the way it does so often in books, so seldom in real life.

On our honeymoon, she is bashful and untried, emerging from the bathroom swathed in hotel-robe cotton. She is wanton, seducing me with the age-old skill of a concubine. She is naked. She wears a vintage corset with red ribbons. She is the woman I will spend the rest of my life loving.

I occupy the minutes between the train's next stop indulging in every fantasy my excited brain can conjure, crossing my legs to hide the evidence of my arousal, avoiding the eyes of my fellow passengers as if they can read my lascivious thoughts and might alert the sleeping woman across from me.

"Tickets. Please have your tickets ready," the conductor calls out.

The train will not make another stop before pulling into Union Station. I make the most of my final moments with today's subject, noting a loose thread on her sleeve and a minuscule scuff on her shoe.

How sweetly her lips curve, when she offers a sleepy smile to the conductor. She presents her ticket —not a monthly pass like mine, but the thin paper of a day ticket. I may never see her again. I feel the loss of her already. I wonder if she might join me for coffee if I asked.

My fantasies become more pedestrian as I think of us walking along the river, talking about books we'd read, our jobs, dreams and the mundane. Perhaps I will ask her on a more formal date. A night at the opera or dinner at one of the fancy restaurants springing up all over the city. She could be the one to break this cycle and set my path on a more righteous one. A happier one.

Her lively brown eyes meet mine, and she bestows a smile upon me. "Excuse me, but do you know which exit I should take to catch a taxi at the train station?"

I frown, lifting a finger to my lips, mimicking the graphic

in the picture over my head. "Shh, this is the Quiet Car."

Hurrying through Union Station, carried along by the herd of people jostling for position on the escalators, I fight an urge to shove someone. But, scanning the crowd, I do not see the one who has caused me to feel so uncharacteristically annoyed. My admonition had sent her scurrying up the train's aisle well ahead of my own exit.

I walk past the food court, taking a briefcase to the ribs with no complaint as someone in a hurry pushes past. Breathing deeply of the mixed odors of Amtrak travelers coming off cross-country jaunts, char-dogs, teriyaki, and cinnamon buns, I begin to calm down. Today will be like any other. The woman on the train has changed nothing.

A young man pushes open the Adams Street door for me to walk through, not to be kind, but because he does not turn back to see that I am right on his heels to avoid having to touch the handle that is surely crawling with germs. Wind blasts my cheeks. Autumn has come early to Chicago, and the air carries the threat of winter in its chill.

"Hey! Mister?"

I do not turn around until I feel the tug at my coat sleeve. People usually don't talk to me, and the homeless beggars have more elaborate routines to get a passerby's attention which I always ignore.

"I'm really sorry about talking in the Quiet Car. I just started riding the train, and I didn't know. I just thought everyone was as sleepy as me!" She laughs, and her brown eyes danced. "Anyway, I wanted to apologize and say I hope I didn't ruin your morning."

Gathering my usual persona around me, after a momentary lapse that twists my face into a perplexed frown, I smile at her. "No problem. Really. I hope I didn't ruin your morning!"

Relief floods her features, and its twin unfurls in my chest.

"Oh, no! Not at all. I'm so glad you told me. You can bet I won't make that mistake again!"

"Then, all is well. I do hope you enjoy the rest of your day," I say, turning to start my normal walk along the river to my office.

"Say, can I buy you a cup of coffee? I'm never going to make it to class on time now anyway."

I smooth another frown as I take in her guileless gaze. No one ever asks me to coffee. I think back to my musings on the train. Where I failed, she has stepped up. Where I only dreamed, she has acted. How bold. How modern. How . . . extraordinary. Perhaps she will be the one after all, the one to change everything.

"That would be lovely. I can show you where to catch a taxi next time, too." I offer her my arm, and we are off.

It is almost like my daydream. Walking over cobblestones, along the olive green river, we talk about ordinary things. She is a student, studying poetry. Unmarried. New to Chicago. No family here, or anywhere else. An orphan, alone, and far too friendly with strangers.

She talks. I listen. I insist on paying at Starbucks, and force a cranberry muffin upon her. She could stand to eat more, I tell her. Chicago winters are rough. "You'll need the extra padding," I say with a wink, earning another laugh.

More relaxed than I have felt in years, half in love with her already, I am still surprised when I make the offer I'd imagined on the train and ask her to dinner. I am even more surprised when she accepts with a smile that borders on flirtatious.

Her address and name are recorded onto a scrap of notebook paper she presses into my hand, and we part.

Ellen. Her name is Ellen Ross. She lives alone in a Berwyn garden apartment. Her only pet is a goldfish. She is allergic to dogs and cats. I am not surprised. I had already noticed the lack of dog hair on her clothing.

The rest of my day is spent in a daze as if she's slipped me a tranquilizer along with her pertinent information. I am shaken at the turn of events, my stomach refusing lunch. I should have lied. I should have told her I am a lawyer, or an investment banker, instead of the truth. Why am I so dull? So ordinary? How did I gain her favor when I am so much older, so obviously awkward, and boring? Insurance! What young, beautiful girl would want to go to dinner with an insurance risk analyst? I wonder if she's having one over on me. If, even now, she's at school laughing with her girlfriends over the stupid old man who paid for her breakfast. Boy, she's sure paid me back for shushing her on the train!

Maybe she is just like all the rest. Or, maybe she is the one I was meant to find, the one I will spend the rest of my life loving. And, though this riddle of a puzzle is new, I relax. Part of the game is trying to piece these things together. When I arrive at her apartment, I will know and be satisfied. A small part of me, previously slumbering, awakens and fills the rest of my day with fantasies of what might bloom between us.

When I arrive to pick her up, promptly at 8:00 o'clock, as agreed, I carry a bouquet of wild flowers and another surprise. I take deep, calming breaths as I wait on the narrow landing outside her door; I free my mind of all expectations, more than willing to take even the shame that will come should this all be a joke.

Still, I must admit to a rush of happiness when she opens her door. "Flowers! That's so nice!" she says, giving me a hug.

When she draws back, and I recover from her smile, and

touch, I see she is wearing a dress. A red, slinky dress. On her feet are black shoes with only a strap over her toes and a high heel in back. She is wearing more makeup than this morning, and her blonde hair is fluffier, falling over her shoulders in rebellious curls. I do not see how she could be wearing panties under such a tight dress, and I imagine her bra is whore-red like the paint she wears on her lips.

I excuse myself when she says she'll put the flowers in a vase, and she shows me her washroom.

Alone, I wash my hands, careful not to touch anything but the handle on the soap dispenser, which I wipe when I finish. I've left the door ajar, so do not have to worry about that. She hadn't noticed the handkerchief I'd wrapped around the cellophane covering the flower stems that I tucked back into my pocket. They never do.

Looking at my reflection in the mirror over her dirty sink, the hopeful part of me that had awakened crawls back into its dark box. Ellen Ross has turned out to be like all the rest after all. My path cannot change. I hush the voice from deep within that tries to tell me otherwise, wiping my weary eyes with the back of my hands.

I spend a moment thinking of the way her pretty brown eyes will change. I picture a variety of expressions on her face, none of which I have seen her wear before. She will scream. She will cry. She will beg until she cannot anymore. She will faint.

I remind myself that what she does is of no concern to me. Not really. She will see the knife, and she will know. Her puzzles will be revealed, and I will be satisfied.

LA BELLE MORT

"Young woman, you do realize, if you could be with child, you may plead your belly?" The judge had tired eyes.

Eliza remained quiet, and the audience tittered.

"Very well. Lady Elizabeth Jane Morton, you are sentenced to be taken hence to the prison in which you were last confined where, after three Sundays have passed, you will be hanged by the neck until dead. May the Lord God have mercy upon your soul."

Gypsy . . . succubus . . . witch—murmurs from the crowd, as she was led away.

Had they looked beyond the snow-white skin, wild black curls, and eerie calm, they would have seen the bones of her knuckles shining through her skin; she held her hands clenched painfully tight to keep from lashing out at all of them and going absolutely mad.

A cell to myself at the end of a narrow, gloomy hall. Dank, always cold. Oozing drips stain the walls rust-brown. Insanity—

cackles, moans, and screams. Fleas, mice, and slithering sounds in the darkness. A cot and rough blanket. A long bench to sit upon. Small comforts from charity Ladies, mercifully none familiar to me. They bring gifts, the smell of perfume, and pity. I accept them all. Today's treasures—ink, quill pens, and paper. Solace found.

Eliza fought slumber; it crawled with dark dreams and beckoned with greedy fingers. Hours, long and black, were spent struggling to cling to awareness, her life dwindling away.

Regrets stung. Time was short, and peace was as elusive as life. Insanity promised everlasting oblivion, and she was tempted to succumb as so many had around her. Writing gave her temporary respite. There was no one to write, so she wrote for herself; poems, thoughts, lists and letters she would never send.

Dear Lord Dover,

Do you sleep peacefully? Do your children fare well without their nursemaid in their nursery? Despite what you have done, my prayers are with their poor little souls.

I wonder where you hid the necklace and if it calls to you in your dreams. Will it haunt you, as surely I will if there is a God and he grants wishes?

My life is forfeit, and still I would rather this death than your wrinkled hands upon me.

Lady Elizabeth Jane Morton

She folded scribbled-upon paper into tiny paper birds and sailed them into the courtyard. Sometimes, they landed in the shadows of the gallows themselves, but usually, the wind caught them and carried them away to join the plentiful refuse littering London's streets.

> *GOOD THINGS*
> *Father*
> *Mayfair House*
> *London*
> *Carriages*
> *Ball gowns*
> *The Waltz*
> *Flirting*
> *James*
> *The Dover children*
>
> *BAD THINGS*
> *This place*

A "new" dress—bodice too tight, tattered skirt. A string to tie my hair off my neck—blessed relief. Small things mean so much now.

She documented everything, writing furiously, clinging to sanity.

A hanging—crowd swelling, sudden, and boisterous, fathers lifting children upon their shoulders, vendors selling meat-pies and posies. It was like a country fair, everyone smiling, fun in the air.

Her mind screamed, *Don't! Look away!* But she was compelled to watch.

They led the prisoner out. His head was down, but Eliza saw the glistening tears on his death-pale flesh. Placed under the gallows, his feet centered atop the wooden trapdoor, he wept openly.

His legs were pinioned, to prevent his soon to be flailing

feet from finding purchase on the brick-lined walls of the famous Long-Drop below. The noose was fitted; a large knot of rope adjusted to rest, just so, beneath his left ear.

The hangman—cloaked in black—the very specter of death. The prisoner wailed—a high-pitched whine—when the hood was placed over his head. Did he open his eyes then, when the cloth covered his face? Did his lashes catch on the fabric, and did he take it in his mouth, dry and musky as he gulped air, grunting and snorting? Did each prisoner have a new hood, or did that frantic man, about to die, smell the deaths that had come before his, lingering in the cloth?

Ghastly, snapping sound ringing out of the pit. Imagined? Surely so; the crowd had cheered when the man fell out of sight.

Life passes too slowly, too quickly. What prayer will save me from this fate?

Eliza was sleeping the first time he came, at dusk.

"Do not be afraid."

She was—trapped in here, weak from lack of real food and sunshine; she was helpless.

The man sat on the narrow bench. He was rather fine looking, his face somewhat stern, and his clothing somber. A cleric, Eliza decided, calming.

"Has that much time passed? It must have, for them to send you."

"I want to help you."

She held back a bitter reply; no one could help her. "I do not believe in God."

"I am the only one you need to believe in." He spread his hands wide as if to dare her to argue that he was anything less than flesh and blood.

Eliza remained silent, and he reached into his pocket,

pulling out a square of paper. He read, "Life passes too slow-ly, too quickly. What prayer will save me from this fate?"

"That is mine!" Eliza bolted from the cot.

Too slow. He tucked the note into the folds of his coat. "Yes, I know."

He handed her another scrap of paper, his fingertips brushing her wrist as it changed hands.

Her cheeks flooded with color, and she escaped his gaze, reading the words on the page.

Proud beauty, angel amidst foul circumstance.
I hear you calling, and know you weep.
Let me guide you in your dark journey, and give you peace in this dread.
In your ruin, find faith in me.

What manner of cleric was this?

"I told you, I do not have faith."

"And I told you, have faith in me."

"I do not understand."

He lifted his hand, tracing the path a tear made down her cheek.

Eliza held very still, quivering under his fingertips.

"You do not have to understand, Lizalamb."

She blinked. He'd called her Lizalamb, just like her fa-ther had a lifetime ago. How odd.

"I'm afraid."

"Of course you are, but you can conquer your fears and all will be well. This I promise. Have faith."

He freed the string she had used to tie her hair back, and reached into his pocket once more.

Red ribbons, bows that give girlish pleasure. His voice gruff as he gifted them. What a strange, fascinating man.

Eliza nibbled on her bottom lip, the treasures clutched in her hand, red ends trailing from her fist. "Will they let me keep them?"

"Yes, Liza. No one will bother you anymore."

"Thank you."

A pail of warm water, beside it—wrapped with care—a whole bar of jasmine scented soap.
Eliza plaited the scarlet ribbons into her hair. She waited, writing.
A stranger, in my darkest hour, offering peace for my faith, scarlet ribbons to tie my hair.

My fate is unchangeable,
measured in rope and wood,
the dozen yards to my doom.
Rise above, fall below.
The silent clock keeps ticking.

Yet, something about him—sanctuary; already, I am anxious for his return, to feel as I did in those brief moments, when his hands held mine.
Hopeful.

Finally, he came.

It was night. She was sleeping.

"Close your eyes." He placed his hand over them.

Eliza struggled, pushing him away.

He let her go, holding up his lantern.

More handsome than remembered. A trick of light or a young girl's heart finding something of desire's fancy in these last days? Lust, peace, comfort. His voice—an anchor in the night.

"You can control your reaction to fear if you control your mind. You need not face the unknown at all if you have a place within yourself of peace and serenity, and a means to find it. Change what you think, and you change what you feel." He opened the little door in the lantern and blew out the flame within. "Close your eyes."

This time she obeyed.

Days, hours, and precious little life left. What is the harm in doing as he asks?

His fingers skimmed her hair. She whimpered, but did not move away.

"Think of a place, familiar, happy, and safe. Go there in your mind. Picture it, smell it, feel it."

Mayfair House—Father, laughter, parties and endless possibilities. Death, ruin, empty, sold.

"I have no safe places."

She was not afraid, though she struggled to find tranquility as memories crashed in on her; she wanted it to continue. She wanted to think of something else. Anything else.

"Then make believe. Tell me where you would be, if you could be anywhere you desired."

His smell—crisply clean, manly under soap. A sudden image—him, standing in a lake, surrounded by a meadow dotted with tansies, forget-me-nots, and lemon balm. The sky above is endless, blue. His hair is loose, dark. He is naked.

"Ahhh," she sighed.

"Tell me."

"No!"

"Why not?"

"Because!"

"This I definitely wish to hear. Tell me." His voice held a

new teasing note that sent prickles down her arms.

"Well," she said, clearing her throat. "I saw a meadow of wildflowers and a lake, bluer than the sky."

"And?"

"You were there."

"Me? What was I doing?"

"You were in the lake."

"Drowning?"

He was not old, but he was not young either. A cleric, surely he had heard lustful thoughts before.

"No, bathing I think."

"Naked?"

"Of course! Clothing would be silly indeed if one were bathing."

"What were you doing, besides watching me?"

"That was all I was doing!"

"No picnic, no flower gathering or cloud watching?"

"Oh yes! We supped on steak and kidney pies, Devonshire cheeses, and exotic fruit sent in from India." She laughed.

"What eclectic tastes you have! Did I kiss you?"

"Oh my . . . yes. We kissed and kissed," she said, her voice dreamy and girlish to her ears.

"And, were you joyful then, Lizalove?"

"Yes. Yes, I was," she answered, faintly surprised.

The next time he came, he carried a rope.

"Is this one of the things you fear?"

"Yes." Her gaze darted to the coil of twine.

He placed it on her lap, the ends snaking to the ground. Her fingers shrunk away.

"Tell me what you fear."

"The way it will feel. The weight of it, the roughness of it, the finality of it."

"Do you trust me?"

What is it about him? I am girlish and hopeful, excited to greet the day because he might fill it. Be he cleric or devil, man or beast, in these last days he gives things believed lost forever. I am drowning, willingly.

"Yes."

He took the rope from her, his fingers lingering over hers. Her flesh tingled, from his hand to her belly, and between her legs.

He made a loop of the rope and hung it around her neck. She did not move.

He bunched up her skirt with one hand and held the rope with the other. She met his gaze and spread her legs wider. She wanted his touch, no matter what that made her, or him.

His hand slid up the rope until his knuckles brushed the skin under her chin. His other hand curled around her inner thigh, fingers walking a silken path. He pinched her and petted her, and she did not move.

"In fear, can be found pleasure, just as in darkness can be found light."

Eliza felt the truth of his words as the rope around her neck tightened, the hemp scratchy. Like whiskers, they licked her. She no longer cared about the rope because of what his other fingers did. Her head lolled back against the wall.

"Do you feel it?" His breath kissed her cheek.

Eliza jutted her hips to his hand.

"Yes." She watched him lick his lips as he slid his fingers into the hot clutch of her body.

"Yes, Lizalove. You feel it." His eyes were obsidian darkness.

Torture—spread wide for him, still, not flinging myself upon him. He gave what was needed yet held back. I know there is more. Twin sighs as fingers pushed inward, curling within. He did not ask about the lack of barrier.

"Is the rope a concern now?"

"No."

Languid, craving the pleasure—forbidden delights. His lips curving against mine, tongue slipping between. Suckling him, an arm looped around his neck, fingers winding in the tangle of his dark hair.

"You can find this place too, anytime you wish. Squeeze your cunnie around my fingers."

Cunnie—a startling word, naughty. I like it and think, had I the time, I might find that I am a very, very bad girl after all.

Her flesh gripped his fingers, and new pleasures bloomed. His thumb nudged high in her cleft, burning.

"Oh God . . . please."

"Yes indeed, Eliza. Soon, soon." He withdrew his fingers.

She started to pull her thighs together, but he stopped her, tightening the rope around her throat.

"Not yet."

She shuddered and stayed spread wide.

"Do you touch yourself in the night, Lizalove? Right there?" His hand cupped her yearning flesh again.

"Yes."

"What do you think of?"

"You." She could not lie to him.

He removed the loop of rope from her neck.

"Think of the darkness, think of the rope, think of my cock," he said.

"Ohhh."

When she opened her eyes, he was gone.

She went straight to bed.

Losing track of time, sun and moon changing places. He has not come back. Found out? Had all he wanted?

Maybe something has happened to him. I do not even know his name.

Wondrous gift. A note from him.

How can this be?
I mourn what is not yet gone!
Emptied by the future that does not hold you.
Do I risk hell for a heaven here and now?
Dare I tempt the rope?
I find you guilty of only one thing, angelic thief; you have taken my heart, and wherever you are,
I know, there shall my heart be too.
Fear not the darkness—I am the dark, and you are my secret, eternal.
I will set you free.
Give all to me.

———

Still, the Cleric does not come.

———

A new visitor. Why am I so afraid when they tell me?

No formal visiting rooms here; charity Ladies, physicians, clerics and visitors all came to the condemned's cell when audience was desired.

Nothing to tidy, no mirror to check, knowing she had never been dirtier or more ashamed, she stood with her cheek pressed to the bars so she could see who the guard led to her.

James Thomas, Lord Dover's gardener and her erstwhile suitor.

Her knees went weak. She crumpled to the dusty floor; the only thing keeping her from falling was her grip on the metal doors of her cell.

Shouldn't she at least be allowed a choice? She was to die. Should she not be given the right to refuse a visitor? She only wished to see the Cleric.

She closed her eyes and, only because she refused to be found by anyone groveling in the dirt, she lifted herself up and was standing when the doors opened.

"James." She wished she had it in her to tell him to leave. Leave now and never come back, never think of her again like this.

James. Sweet, sweet boy.

"Eliza, I came as soon as they would allow it!"

He did not offer his hand or a hug, and that was not surprising. His courtship had been most proper. It was not in his nature to be overly demonstrative.

James Thomas had an innocence about him that still tugged at Eliza's heartstrings, though she was not in love with him. On the Dover estates, their paths had crossed often. She spent much of her time out of doors with the children, and James was always to be found rallying the score of servants who attended to Lord Dover's expansive gardens wherever the family was in residence.

She had gently rebuffed his overtures, her heart still wounded over her father's death and the sudden changes in her life without him, though a part of her had started to warm. James was so sweet, good and kindly. He would make someone a very fine husband, she'd started to think.

"You should not have come." She started to say more, but realized that was all there really was to say. Anything they might have had was best forgotten. He should go. She turned away from him.

"I had to come! They have not found Lady Dover's necklace. Lord Dover says if you wish to return home, you know what to do. I guess he means tell them where you hid it, but you can't have done what they say. Not you. You're good, Eliza, I just know it." His brown eyes softened, though worry bracketed them with a thicket of frown lines.

Lord Dover had sent him. Sent James to tell her to acquiesce to his demands. For, that was what his coded message meant. Sleep with me. Be my Mistress and all will be forgotten. You can come home again.

Could he really do that, she wondered. Have the Court reverse her sentence? Yes. She supposed a man as powerful as Lord Dover, who had managed to get her convicted of theft without any evidence, could do that.

All she would have to do was sleep with him. Not just once, for that she may have been able to stomach, but many times, for as long as he desired her. She would have to let the old man do anything he wished with her, or it would be back to prison.

When her father died, and Lord Dover had offered her the post as nursemaid to his brood, he had seemed so kindly, her father's old friend, sympathetic to her loss and change of status. With nowhere else to turn, she had gratefully accepted the position.

Very soon, it became apparent that the old man had motives other than kindliness. His pursuit of her had been relentless. After he tried to sneak into her chambers one night, despite having nowhere to go, Eliza had been on the verge of fleeing when he had sprung the theft trap, and had her arrested.

He had made her the same offer before the authorities had arrived to take her away. *Sleep with me. Be my Mistress, and all will be forgotten.*

"James, you may tell Lord Dover I did not take the necklace." She would still rather die than be his plaything.

"Eliza! There must be a way to stop this nonsense. You cannot hang for something you did not do!" Emotion seemed to overcome him, and he reached for her hand, which she allowed him to hold for a moment before gently pulling away.

"I thank you for coming, but you should go now."

"I wanted us to marry, you know," his voice broke when he spoke.

"James, you barely know me. You need to forget about me."

"How can I? I love you." He made to reach for her again, and she moved away, unable to face the pain in his gentle brown eyes.

Once she had dreamed of love, of marriage. Once, life had held promise. Back then, she would have rebuffed this boy's advances, preferring to dally with the affections of older, richer men. The spoiled daughter of a Lord, she had her pick, sure she would settle one day on the right match.

"James, I do not love you. I am a Lady, and you are a gardener. Nothing changes that. You and I were never meant to be together. Had my circumstance been different, I would not have deigned even to speak with you." Harsh words, meant to hurt, though not entirely true, for she had always been nice to everyone. Words designed to send him away, and think of her no more.

"How can you say that? You were always so kind. So nice." His look of bemused hurt almost made her stop.

"Like I told you before; you never really knew me at all. Now, go. Please. Deliver my message to Lord Dover, and forget all about me."

"Eliza!"

"Guard! He's ready to leave." She did not watch as he was taken away, and would not have seen even had she looked. Tears flooded her vision and choked her breathing.

Though she had not loved James, in him she had glimpsed

the possibility of a future, of a life without her father that, while different, would be livable. Sending him away, she finally allowed herself to mourn the loss of her life. Her tears did not stop for days. More than once, she was tempted to give into Lord Dover's demands so that she might live.

And still, the Cleric did not return.

I would give him anything. My dreams are filled with images of him, naked in the darkness. He is all I have left. He is all I desire.

When she woke the moon was high, and he was there. He stood near the window. Beyond him, she saw falling snowflakes.

She moved to one side of the cot, telling him in the action exactly what she wanted from him.

He was upon her before she could let out a breath. He pulled up her skirt and they crashed together. Their mouths clung, and their hands clutched. His whiskers abraded her skin. She arched into the pain of it, needing him with a violence that was frightening.

He ran his hands slowly over her body. Eliza thought he meant to be tender then, and did not want his kindness. She wrapped her fingers around his arms, her torn nails ripping into his flesh, dragging him down to her.

He fisted his hands in her hair and yanked her into place beneath him. She spread her legs wide, welcoming him like the whore she had been called.

He devoured her mouth, leaving it only to lick his way to her nipples, biting and sucking them through the bodice of her dress until she moaned, forcing him to clasp his hand over her mouth. He undid his trousers. She felt the heat of him slide into her. There was no pain, only a sense of fullness, and pleasure.

He rose over her, propping himself up upon his hands. She opened her mouth to lick a corded muscle in his arm. A droplet of sweat seeped from his skin, and she savored its salt on her tongue.

She came, in a flood—sudden, harsh and sweet—and then so did he, lifting himself out of her, stroking his cock as he knelt between her thighs, shooting his seed onto her belly.

"Lizalove." He kissed the bruises his passion had left upon her.

"I do not even know your name." She rubbed his release into her flesh.

"William."

"Thank you, William."

Another day.

"There is one more thing, Liza."

She nodded.

I will give him anything he wishes for, and not ask a single question. I will do anything he wants; this is all I will ever have.

He wrapped his fingers around her throat, his other hand delving between her thighs.

"Hold your breath, Lizalove. Do not breathe for as long as you can, until you grow dizzy."

William kissed her, pushing his breath into her mouth, showing her how to breathe, slowly and deeply. She took his breath into her body, holding it when he squeezed her throat. It was difficult, not gasping for air, not panting with lust, but she looked into his eyes, and found euphoria in the control he showed her. She went with him to the place he had shown her, the peaceful meadow. His fingers worked magic, and her body opened for his bunched, fucking fingers.

Before it was over, he pushed his cock into her, choking her as he took her. He came flooding into her body just as she was overtaken by darkness.

"Breathe," he said, giving her his own breath until hers returned to normal.

He held her. "I wish I could do more," he said, as she closed her eyes to shut out everything but him. "Just remember, there is always light, after the darkness. Always."

And for the first time, Eliza believed.

They came for her later, the hangman's assistant and the warden.

They tied her hands behind her back and led her into the morning sun. Her feet made clumsy imprints in the blanket of blinding white snow. The air was crisp and cold. Eliza saw her breath—a warm fog of life she walked through before she closed her eyes.

The crowd cheered, but she was far away, at a pristine lake, with a man who loved her. Flowers bloomed all around them, and she wore red ribbons in her hair.

Under the gallows, she breathed deeply, calmly, until peace flooded her. She opened her eyes again when the hangman placed his hand upon her shoulder.

Eliza looked into his eyes—death's eyes, the hangman's eyes, William's eyes.

"Have faith," she heard him whisper.

Then there was only darkness.

BREAK GLASS IF BROKEN

I should have known better. I should have stayed home, remained alone. I should have known better.

Once you are an adult, every story begins in the middle. Mine is no different. The unpleasant details of what had come before do not need sharing, though they had brought me to New York where I could hide. My job allowed me to disappear. A copy editor's work is essential, yet never as important as that of the writer. This suited me.

In a gray, padded cubicle, reliable words and rules of usage occupied my monitor or filled the space on rectangular pages. Boxed in, I was invisible. Safe. Alone.

Weeknights, I rode the subway to a tiny square apartment with metal bars on the windows and sealed myself behind a door fitted with five deadbolts. I watched the world on television or read about it online. I ate my frozen meals from plastic or cardboard containers and owned no silverware or china, no knives to cut. No glass or china to break. I possessed nothing I did not consider disposable.

Weekends, I wandered museums where I could lose myself in the crowds. Walking beside handsome students, listening to docent lectures, I took notes as if I belonged in their cozy, boisterous groups. I fell into step beside family units, close enough to smell the baby-fresh scent of the shampoo mothers used on children's hair. So close that, when the crowd swelled along with my need for contact, my hand could drift over a father's fingers as he held his child's hand upon an escalator or railing.

I reached for elevator buttons at the same time others did, on purpose, knowing my shrugged and smiled apology would be accepted. Knowing those I accosted would not suspect my longing for the touch of another's hand on mine, however fleeting or unwanted.

Listening to strangers' conversations, I would pretend they spoke to me, composing witty replies no one ever heard.

"So, like, the thing about acting is that, like, you can be anyone, you know? Like, I could be a warrior princess, or like a vampire and shit. Clothes, makeup, and attitude are everything, you know? I took dance too, so my coach says I have a really good shot at getting a part real soon."

"Does he say that when you're sucking his dick, or after?" her friend replied as I applauded, silently.

I could blame drama girl for what happened, but I would know it had been my idea, my fault. What if I acted, I had thought. What if instead of acting like one of these vapid young girls, or pretending to be a doctor on a television show, or a cat in a play, I acted as if I was normal? As if I was not damaged. As if I was not afraid.

Though, at first, I comforted myself pretending I had carefully thought the scheme over for weeks, I actually began formulating plans even then, noting the shabby hooker-like clothing these girls sported, casting my gaze around with newfound interest in what others wore, how others acted. Would I be a woman who wore crisp, black suits or one who wore dark-washed, pressed jeans? Did I wish to be no-nonsense in kick-ass leather boots, or flirty in sandals with sky-high heels? Was I the sort of woman who wore dresses with no panties, or one who never carried a purse? Would I be bright as sunshine, cool as spring rain or would I have a metallic tang, like a penny on the tongue?

"Excuse me?" I said to a woman at my office soon after.

Only Botox, I suspected, kept her brow from furrowing at me for bothering her. "Yes? What?"

"I love that suit, and your shoes, and scarf and, well, just everything you have on." My palms sweat. It was the most I had said to anyone, anywhere, since suffering through the interview required to land my job. "Where do you shop?" I forged on, braver now that the words were out, though she stared at me as if I had lost my mind. Maybe I had.

"SoHo or the Lower East has the best boutiques for accessories. Fifth Avenue for serious clothes and shoes. I don't remember where I bought everything, but the suit's Ann Taylor."

I watched her and others like her, until I had a list. Until I knew just who I wanted to be.

> Suit – gray, skirt just above the knee, slim
> fitted jacket, pants with no pleats, low on
> the hips, falling just so (tailoring a must
> for correct length with shoes)
>
> Shoes – sling-back, heels (not too high
> or too short), leather, expensive, pointy
>
> T-shirts – cut simply but made of real-
> ly good cotton or silk, snug fitting, boat
> neck
>
> Belt – wide or skinny (I still couldn't fig-

ure that one out), expensive, metal clasp
Bag – red or another color, expensive
Simple, gold jewelry

Trench coat – black, good material, not
too heavy

Scarves – the only patterns allowed.
Nothing loud or flashy

Very sexy lingerie under it all (this I
guessed), expensive

It was not easy or pleasurable, finding these items, but soon I had them all. I ate Top Ramen and hot dogs for a month, but now I owned something sharp. Heels.

At work, I continued to wear shapeless shift dresses and cardigans, pants that sagged at the knees and sensible flats. No one commented on the new blonde highlights in my hair, worn in my customary, messy bun; maybe no one noticed. Nor did anyone notice the injections that plumped my lips and smoothed my frown lines, or my skin, tinted self-tanner gold. I remained invisible, or so I thought. This was my first mistake, but mistakes are like lies; they always multiply. The first ones are easy and often go unnoticed.

"Hello, my name is Susan. Hello, my name is Frances. Hello, I'm Briana," I practiced in front of my bathroom mirror. "Yes, I'd love a drink. No, I am waiting for someone. Why don't you just fuck off? Fuck me."

The more I practiced, the more I realized it was true; I could be anyone I wanted to be, anyone I wanted people to think I was.

"I'm a writer. I write erotica. I write romance novels. I am an editor, a doctor, a lawyer. I head up an investment firm in Paris. I live in Tribeca. I am from Milan, Japan, Italy, here on business. No, I don't want to talk about it. I want you to fuck me."

A woman who wants to get laid, and presents herself as someone without baggage, without strings attached, can find a man to do the deed just about anywhere. I wasn't stupid. I knew better than to go into singles bars, or bad parts of town. I avoided places sure to attract the despondent, the alcoholic, motorcycle riders, or those with prison records, tattoos, or facial piercings. I was in the market for a very specific type of man. I needed a man too nice to come looking for me later, too nice to hurt me, too nice to say no. The sort of man who was clean and carried condoms with him.

The bar at The Ritz Carlton, near Wall Street, the Stock Exchange, and Battery Park was perfect. The restaurant made a nice cover. The setting meant I didn't have to be from New York, yet many people who frequented the place lived in the up- and-coming neighborhood or were tourists themselves.

Drinking from a martini glass, I tipped the bartender generously. He knew, no matter what I ordered, to fill my glass with nothing more than water. A twist of lemon rind completed the illusion. All night, that first time, I sat and picked at a Blackberry, frowned at galley proofs, and fended off would-be suitors. I tried all my stories, all my names, but told all the men (and a few women), "No," until he walked in.

He was the Ken to my Barbie, the scratch to my itch. I knew it, and he knew it. Watching us, anyone would have thought we'd arranged to meet there, were husband and wife, lovers, friends. My knees parted slightly in welcome. He slid into the spot I created for him as if he belonged. "Hello, pretty."

"Hi, handsome," I replied.

"Say you have a room." He did not touch me with his hands, but his strong thighs eased my knees wider apart, and his eyes caressed the newly exposed expanse of my legs.

"I will, once you check in."

"Perfect. I'll be right back." Before he left, he turned his shoulder to the room, slid his hand under my skirt, and cupped my cunt through soaked silk panties. The bartender looked away.

My heart pounded. It was happening. He had touched me. I had been cool, calm, a woman of the world. I didn't even know his name! He didn't know mine. No stories had been required. We would fuck. I would leave. Perfect.

"You don't have to do that, you know," the friendly bartender said to me many weeks later.

By now, I'd grown into my power, and my autonomy. I'd relaxed. My second mistake or maybe my third. I'm losing count.

Giving the bartender only the coolness of my gaze as a reply, I turned back to the room, and that's when it happened. My make-believe world turned into a house of cards, and I knew I had made a terrible error.

"Vera," my boss said briskly as if we had arranged to meet.

Alarm fluttered against my ribs, as violent as the wings of a dying bird trapped in a cage. "Mr. Blunt."

Under his stern brows, steely blue eyes watched as I gathered my trappings of confidence and returned them to my bag. I chewed my bottom lip until his frown stopped me.

He tossed a large bill onto the bar top. Shame flooded my stomach until I realized it was meant for the bartender, not for what was to come. What I would do.

I followed him, swallowing my questions. What did it matter how he knew, how long he had known or why he'd come for me now? We both knew what I pretended to be was, at heart, no act. We both knew I wanted it.

In the elevator, he pushed me to my knees and let me nuzzle my cheek to his custom tailored, wool suit covered cock. Before my eyes closed, his wedding band winked at me.

Of course, no one else boarded the elevator, and the hallway was empty when we alighted.

"Crawl," he said, so I did.

The carpet bit my nylon covered knees, and I felt the burn of scrapes as they formed. There would be blood. As there should be.

The spacious gold-and-green room behind the door he opened boasted a sweeping view of the water surrounding the Statue of Liberty. Harbor view rooms came with their own telescopes. Handy for the voyeur and stargazer alike, I imaged the marketing copy boasting.

Though he did not pay me, I was his whore. Though he did not ask it of me, I gave him everything left of that girl in the bar. He kissed the tears I wept for her away, and held my hands above my head as he grunted over me.

I should have known better, stayed home, and remained alone. I should have known better, and now I do.

Every story should begin at the end; the unpleasant details of what came before do not need sharing. Mine had brought me to the mountains of Colorado, where I could hide.

Working from home, in an office with walls painted uncertain gray, reliable words and rules of usage occupy my monitor. Boxed in, I am invisible. Safe. Alone.

VACANCY

Oliver Ripley fled his youth, riding a bus. His future rushed toward him as he abandoned his past. Boredom and cautious optimism seduced him into fractured daydreams. Anything seemed possible, but what was to come shimmered just out of his imagination's reach like the heat mirages that danced on the asphalt before the Greyhound bus mowed them down.

The first passenger to disembark, Oliver inhaled the odors of the Chicago bus station—diesel fuel, hot rubber, and corn dogs. He slung his duffle bag over his shoulder and walked out onto the busy sidewalk. The world waited, poised to spread wide before him.

No one paid him any attention. He was just another stranger in the nameless crowd. Hurrying people jostled him and did not stop to apologize. The bum he gave a dollar to didn't even say thank you.

When his back ached from the weight of his bag, he checked into a small hotel, drawn to its red sign—VACAN-CY. One C flashed, strobe-like. He paid for a week and settled into room 222. It smelled like cigar smoke and mildew.

The bed was lumpy under a burnt-orange colored bedspread.

Propping open the window with the bible he found in the bedside table, he sat on the broken air conditioner and listened to sirens and traffic. He was happy but restless. Tomorrow was going to be the first day of the rest of his life, and he was eager for it to begin.

A little after midnight, he left the hotel looking for a breeze and distraction.

It was a real scorcher, record setting according to the headline on the newspaper he bought from a corner store. No one talked to him, not even the store clerk who took his money without turning away from CNN. Oliver might have been invisible, and he did not mind at all. He relished the mounting sense of hovering in the night—just an anonymous instant in time—his future about to be. Fate would take him where he needed to go. The air hummed with potential.

He was lost, but not concerned, when he sensed the vampire girl standing against a wall outside a nightclub. A line of people waited between blue-velvet ropes next to the building, but Oliver barely noticed them; his senses were too full of the potent signal the vampire cast off.

Her hair was black, the jagged ends tipped with cherry-pink. She lifted her chin and pushed a lock of hair behind one ear, meeting his gaze. Her eyes glowed like polished emeralds, reflecting the neon club-lights. When she stepped away from the wall and walked toward him, he saw her eyes were calmer in color like a pond back home in Indiana.

Oliver shivered and pushed a flicker of unease away. He was a Ripley; a vampire hunter. He could do this. If she talks to me, my future starts right now.

"Are you lost?" she asked.

Not anymore. "Maybe a little." He stepped closer, catching her perfumed scent. "Do you know where the Admiral

Arms Hotel is? I think on 63rd?"

She laughed and took him by the hand as if they hadn't just met. "You checked into a hotel and don't know where? Come on. I'll take you. The streets here are dangerous at night." She wiggled her eyebrows, pierced with silver hoops on both sides.

She was petite, barely reaching his chin, even in her high-heeled boots. The thought of her protecting him was ridiculous, but he squeezed her hand and walked with her, letting her lead him deeper into his destiny. He wondered if she could feel it opening before them like a shadowy cave ready to be explored.

"What's your name?" he asked in a casual tone. One mistake could give her the upper hand.

"Cire." Her thumb stroked his palm.

"Mine's Oliver."

"Like the orphan in that book? I read it in high school. You know the one I mean?"

"Yeah. Dickens," he said, faintly impressed she knew the reference.

"How perfect." She grinned, still seemingly unaware of the danger she was in.

"Why, because I'm lost?" He smiled down at her, matching her easygoing vibe.

"Not lost. Found. I found you. Finders keepers, losers weepers." She looked pleased with herself.

"It's my birthday tomorrow. Today." He wasn't into birthdays, but he wanted to keep her talking. Keep her distracted.

"Well, happy birthday then, Stranger. How old are you?"

"Twenty-two."

"And you're all alone?" She looked up at him and licked her full, red-painted lips.

He thought he could see her calculations, her plotting and planning, as her gaze moved over his face.

"Not alone. With you. Kept. Remember?" He smiled again, easing the growing sense of anticipation and danger that seemed to snap in the air around them.

They didn't talk the rest of the way. The silence was peaceful. Back home everyone talked too much. Always telling him what to do. What not to do. Who to be. How to be.

VACANCY, the hotel sign still read, one C blinking.

"May I come up?" she asked, as if it were the most natural thing in the world.

Surprised at how easy this was, Oliver reminded himself that things would be different now, his family's special rules for him left behind. He was already proving himself as capable as the rest of them, and he almost wished they were here to see it.

"Sure," he said, careful to keep his tone as relaxed as Cire's, turning his thoughts back to the business at hand.

They climbed the stairs after discovering the elevator decorated with an OUT OF ORDER sign.

Signs were everywhere. Something magical was in the air; he felt it. He almost asked if Cire did too, but he didn't want to alarm her when his seduction was going so well.

After he hung the DO NOT DISTURB sign on the doorknob and locked the heavy deadbolt, he turned and watched the vampire girl wander around the small room. She didn't seem to notice the faint outline on the wall where the mirror had hung before he'd removed it and put it in the closet.

"Do you have any weed?" She sat on the edge of the bed, tugging off her boots. Her toenails were painted sky-blue.

"No. I don't do drugs." Drugs, along with dating, had been discouraged by his family, along with so many other things. Normal things. But that was behind him now; for the first time in his life, Oliver was free to do whatever he wanted.

"Cool. Just say no and all." She walked to him and looped her arms around his neck. Her gaze was hazy. Her eyelids drooped.

She still seemed to see him as nothing more than her latest meal, unaware she'd stepped into a vampire hunter's trap and was already under his spell.

He kissed her. It was like dipping his face into a mountain stream. Her tongue was velvety and cooler than the night air. Though it was his first time, Oliver knew what to do. He pulled her short black dress over her head, curling his fingers under its pleated hem. Cire was naked underneath. Her skin was alabaster-white, her breasts small and up tilted.

"This is crazy," he said, cupping her breasts, slipping under waves of lust. He reminded himself not to get too carried away.

She tugged his zipper down, reaching inside his jeans and curling her fingers around his erection. "Let me." Her voice was hoarse.

She sank to her knees, pulling down his jeans as she went. Her hot mouth closed on his cock. She slithered her lips down the shaft.

Pleasure made Oliver's knees buckle, and he groped for the wall behind him.

She glanced up at him with those remarkable green eyes, and he looked away, afraid she would see the triumph in his eyes betraying his excitement. He was like an actor about to step on the stage for the first time after waiting in the wings, hidden in the shadows. He was no longer the disappointment in a family full of standouts. Tonight, he was the man he'd been destined to be—a powerful vampire hunter like the rest of the Ripleys. He was becoming everything he was meant to be because of Cire. She was his destiny. Did she feel it too? Or did she still think she was the one seducing him?

He watched her, hypnotized by the slow bobbing of her

head. A strand of saliva shimmered like a spider web when she stopped, connecting them as she sat back on her heels. She licked her lips, and the thread snapped.

She stood and slid her fingers into his hair, pushing the tousled brown layers away from his temples. "You're so fine." Her lips moved against his neck.

He lifted her and put her back to the wall, leaning into her, holding her up. Sliding his hands under her ass, he guided himself into her hot, welcoming body. Their skin was slippery, weeping sweat, making lewd sucking sounds as they surged together and came apart.

She wound her legs around his waist. Her back thudded against the wall with each thrust.

Oliver wondered if it was possible to fuck someone so hard their bones shattered, but he didn't stop. It felt too good, everything he'd thought it would be.

She tightened her legs around him. Her muscles convulsed as she began to come, and Oliver was lost to the exquisite heat shuddering snugly around him, milking him dry.

Oliver fell into the abyss thankfully, willingly. Was death like this, a complete letting go, an escape? For her sake, he hoped so. Surprised by the unexpected flicker of compassion he felt for the vampire girl, he didn't let it stop him from doing what he'd been born to do.

Around them, the air grew heavier and seemed to pulse as their spirits crashed together in orgasmic bliss. His hunter's soul reached out and captured her vampire spirit just as her sharp teeth brushed his throat. Before it was over, and she went limp in his arms, he saw the dawning in her beautiful green eyes when she realized what he was. He soothed her with tender kisses as she began to die in a ritual as old as time.

"It's all right. It will be over soon," he whispered.

Shuddering against him, she gave into the inevitable.

In the morning, he was tired. Thinking was like reading a book with a stocking over his head—blurry, suffocating and annoying. He had a nagging feeling he forgot important things in the light of a new day.

He reflected on one blazingly clear moment from the night before, an odd wave of fear, right in the middle of things. Oliver had been looking down at Cire. Her pale skin glowed, ghostly, bruised and marked from his use of her body. She'd appeared strong enough to take it, readily capable of stealing a foolish man's life. Yet, just as he'd felt the vampire hunter rise inside of him, ready to take her out before she could kill him, he'd doubted himself. Wondered if they were right, and he would prove too weak.

Now, he was troubled. What if fate hadn't guided him at all? Maybe he'd taken a wrong turn on the dark streets, and he was the one meant to die that night.

Last night, he'd ridden a seesaw of lust and uncertainty, confidence and terror. His recollection of events was filled with black spots he could not illuminate, no matter how hard he tried. Something sinister seemed to creep along the edge of his memories, and he wondered—if he could move his head quickly enough—if he might come face to face with it and be scarred forever.

Despite one strange, fear-filled moment, everything had turned out all right. He'd proven himself. His future was secure; his brother was coming and was sure to be satisfied with what Oliver had done.

Oliver pushed his worry aside. He had been lost, but now he was found. He had not known for sure which way to go in life, and Cire had shown him the way. As a boy, he had believed his vampire-slayer family was immoral, but now he knew they were just.

No one in the family had thought Oliver had it in him, especially his older brother. No one had faith in him—the black sheep, the nothing in Jonathan Ripley's shadow. How wrong they'd been.

Oliver arranged the vampire girl upon the bed, drawing the ugly orange blanket back, presenting her on the plain sheets instead. Her skin glowed with the iridescence of pearls against the ivory cotton. Her crimson-pink streaked hair flowed like a fiery river over the pillows, and her green eyes adored him, even in death.

She was so beautiful. It hurt to look at her. He turned away, listening to the sounds of his new city pulsing outside.

Oliver was no longer anxious or afraid; his future was happening now. He was a vampire hunter.

*This story continues in *Immoral: Tales of a Vampire Hunter #1*, *Depraved: Tales of a Vampire Hunter #2*, and *Bespelled: Tales of a Vampire #3* available at your favorite bookseller.

RANDOM FACTS ABOUT ZANDER VYNE

because bios are boring

I used to let people think Zander was a he, to sell more stories, and because it was fun having a penis (even if imaginary, those things are the shit).

Unusual talents – drunken palm-reading and Improv story-spinning (usually not at the same time)

Fears – big ass spiders (because, really . . . a spider in your ass is scary as fuck); Bad punctuation (recurrent nightmares about it creeping into finished books)

Loves – weird people, head-banging music (extra points if made by a woman), sailing (lived on a sailboat for five years), used-book stores

Best job I ever had- (besides writing, which is not a job, but a love) working in a movie theater

NOTE FROM ZANDER VYNE

Dear Reader,

Thanks for buying this book, and for supporting the short-story format.

Honest, not paid for, reader reviews really do matter, so please take a moment to tell me if you enjoyed *Amaranthine Rain* by writing a review wherever you bought the book or by sending me an email: zandervyne@gmail.com

All my best,

Zander Vyne

P.S. If email is not your thing, connect with me on Twitter, Facebook, Tumlr, Pinterest or www.zandervyne.com.

Other Books
by Zander Vyne

Immoral: Tales of a Vampire Hunter #1

Depraved: Tales of a Vampire Hunter #2

Bespelled: Tales of a Vampire Hunter #3